The Baronet from Bombay

Reluctant Titles, Volume 2

Amanda Panhorst

Published by Amanda Panhorst, 2022.

This is a work of fiction. Similarities to real people, places, or events are entirely coincidental.

THE BARONET FROM BOMBAY

First edition. May 13, 2022.

Copyright © 2022 Amanda Panhorst.

Written by Amanda Panhorst.

The Baronet from Bombay

By Amanda Panhorst

1

Prologue

"You have to," the boy said.

"No, I don't," replied the girl.

Harry snorted his unbelief in response. "That's what girls do. They get married."

"We don't all have to," Gussie insisted. "And I shall not. Not ever."

"I would," Rosy said. "If only I could choose—"

"You cannot marry one of your father's grooms, Rose," Gussie said with some exasperation. "It doesn't matter how handsome you think he is."

Rosy huffed. "Then I shall never marry either." She picked herself up from the grass where the three children lay. "Even under the tree, it is too hot. I'm going to see my pony."

Harry and Gussie watched their friend saunter off in the direction of her beloved pony, then settled in to the grass of the field, heads cradled in their hands, and continued their cloud watching. Gussie, finding no shapes or images of import in the sky, sighed and reached a hand down for the leather-bound book by her side. She brought it up above her head, trying to find her place.

"Aren't you going to ask if I'll get married?" Harry said.

"No."

"Good. Because my answer is no, too. Not for the world."

Gussie replied only with a disinterested hum and kept to her book. She could feel Harry's eyes on her, but the subject of marriage had become boring to her the moment she had proclaimed her intentions against the institution.

A pause of about a minute placed itself between the two children. Gussie was just settling into her book of prints and sketches of the animals of Brazil, when a stirring beside her warned that Harry was not done talking. She lifted an annoyed brow, waiting.

"Why don't you want to marry?" he asked.

"Because I don't want a husband. I want to read."

"*Couldn't you read after you marry?*"

"*Not as much. Mama never does. Do you ever see your mother reading?*"

A pause. "*Yes, when the post comes.*"

"*That does not count.*"

"*Why not? Reading is reading, isn't it? Who cares if it's a letter or a book?*"

"*It's not just reading, it's...learning. Studying. Like Papa says they do at Cambridge and Oxford.*"

"*But you can't go to either of those places. Girls aren't allowed.*"

"*Perhaps they would let me if I studied enough. But that can only happen if you will allow me to read and stop talking about silly marriage.*"

Harry grunted and resumed his study of the clouds. A few minutes passed in silence, but sure enough, Harry made as if to speak again. Gussie lowered her book and waited.

"*I might marry you.*"

A surprised cry escaped her. She dropped her book onto her chest and looked at him. "*Me? Well, that's impossible. I just told you I won't ever marry. Stop being so stupid.*"

"*Well, if I had no other option but to marry, if there was nothing I could do about it, I'd marry you. That's all.*"

Gussie gave this some thought. "*I wouldn't be a good wife. I'd make sure of it. You would tire of me so quickly that you would send me away. But I would take all your books with me as payment for having to be your wife.*"

"*Suits me. We only have a few, and I don't want 'em,*" *he replied.* "*But what if you father says you have to marry someone? Would you then? Who would it be?*"

Gussie cast up her eyes, thoroughly done with the subject. "*The day I marry is the day you inherit Camrose!*"

Harry reared his head back against his hands and gave her a look of utter confusion. "Inherit Cousin Howard's house? George gets it. He's his son. Why would I inherit it?"

"Your name and John's name are in their family Bible. I saw them when I snuck into the library at Camrose during the last picnic. After George, your brother John would inherit, and after John, you would inherit."

"Really? How come I never knew that?"

"Probably because you don't read and have never looked in your family Bible." Gussie said, taking up her book again.

Harry was calculating in his head, that was clear. She hoped she could get another two pages in before he spoke again but underestimated his powers of comprehension. "That would mean that three people would have to die before I got Camrose."

"Dismal, isn't it?"

"That means John would have to die too. Pff, that will never happen. He'll live forever just so he can annoy me for the rest of my life."

"Then you have nothing to worry about."

"Neither do you, I reckon."

"What do you mean?"

Harry rolled onto his side to look at her more easily. "If you're serious, you'll never have to marry because I'll never have Camrose."

"Precisely."

"Well then, let's make a pact. So we each keep our word."

"Our word? What do you mean?"

Harry rolled away from her and reached over for his jacket lying next to him on the grass, digging into a pocket. "You said you would never marry unless I get Camrose. I said I'd marry you if I didn't have any other choice." He rolled back over to her with his pocket knife in his hand. "Well, if I got Camrose, I'd have to get married, wouldn't I?"

Gussie thought a moment, after which she said slowly, "Yes. When a man owns a house, he has to have a wife to keep it."

"So," he continued, "If I ever have Camrose, I'll marry you to keep it for me."

"But you never will inherit Camrose."

"I know, but if I do, then we'll both be getting what we promised: you'll marry me because I'll have inherited Camrose, like you said, and I'll marry you, because I'll have to. You see? So, we'll promise each other with a blood pact to keep our word. Make it official."

Gussie narrowed her eyes at him. "You are po...popa...poprosterous!" She thought she had that right. She had only discovered that word the day before. "It will never happen. Very well."

She put her book next to her and lifted herself up into a sitting position. "How do you make a blood pact? It had better not involve that knife."

"Of course it involves the knife. I thought you were clever," Harry said. He situated himself next to her and hovered the knife over the palm of his hand. "We each draw blood and then we mix it, promising that we'll keep our word at the same time."

"I am not going to make myself bleed."

"I'll do it for you, if you like."

"No!" Gussie cried, snatching her hands to her chest.

"It's not going to hurt, I promise. It doesn't have to be a big prick. Look here, I'll do it first so you'll see."

Gussie drew back a little but could not help watching as Harry pressed the knife to his open hand. Nothing happened. Scowling, Harry pressed harder. Still nothing.

"Huh," he said, raising the knife to examine it. Before Gussie could suggest some other way of binding their souls over nonsensical circumstances, he fell to poking his hand all over with the knife.

"Harry, stop," she said, wishing she were brave enough to snatch the knife away from him, but at the same time pleased with herself that she wasn't that stupid.

As he continued, Harry began to laugh. "How dull this thing is! I guess I've never sharpened it. It will never work, see—ouch! Perhaps it was sharp enough."

As the blood flowed from the cut on the top of his hand, Gussie cast her eyes up to the sky and wondered, not for the first time, how a boy two years older than her could still be so foolish. Couldn't he, at eleven, act as grown up as she was at nine?

But that really was a lot of blood. At least, she thought so. Her stomach gave an unpleasant turn. "Don't just sit there, put your handkerchief to it, do!"

Harry, who had been twisting his hand this way and that to direct the trickles of blood to his liking, looked at his jacket lying on the grass. "I didn't bring one."

"Heavens," she murmured as her stomach roiled again. She screwed her eyes shut and dug into the pocket of her dress, producing her own handkerchief. "There, bind it up, quick."

"You're not going to be ill, are you? It's just a scratch, maybe...ouch."

"Tell me when I can open my eyes."

She heard Harry mumble something about girls and their fragility when it came to gore but kept her eyes firmly closed.

"You can look now."

She opened one disdainful eye to see Harry, his hand now covered, holding the knife out to her. "Your turn. Do you want help?"

She glared at him. "Are you mad?" She snatched the knife from his outstretched hand, ready to instruct him on the proper way to conduct a blood pact she had herself only just found out about. "You could have just done this, watch."

She placed the tip of the knife to the pad of her first finger, pressed and twisted it until it produced a tiny droplet of blood. "See? No more than a prick of a needle. I've done it a hundred times sewing my samplers."

"I don't sew," Harry said flatly.

"Now what?"

"Now, we mix our blood together and make a promise. Put your finger on my hand."

"Oh, Harry, no."

"That's how it works. You said you'd do it. Come on, then."

Taking a deep breath and holding it, she reached her hand over to Harry as he uncovered his wound, which was certainly a bit more than 'just a scratch.' She shut her eyes. "You do it."

She felt his fingers, rather grubby ones, close around her own. Then the warmth and pressure on the tip of her finger as he pressed it against his hand. "Now swear. Promise that we'll marry each other if I should ever get Camrose."

"I promise. If you inherit Camrose, we'll get married."

"I swear it too."

He released her hand. "There. That's it. We've done ourselves a good thing. Now we don't have to worry about ever getting married."

Gussie shifted away from him and his gore and rose to go. She needed to get away from that blood. "I am never doing that again," she said as she walked away.

"You don't have to," Harry called after her. "Nothing can break a blood pact."

Chapter One

Rutland, England, 1814

"Look."

The voice of her friend brought Gussie's mind, which had been swirling round a particularly confusing passage in her reading of Plato the night before, back to her present situation: astride her horse walking down a lane in Rutland on a brisk November morning.

Only a handful of things could entice Augusta Stilwell from staying curled up in bed with a book this early in the morning, and a morning ride with Rosy Barrett was one of them. A groom followed five or six lengths behind them.

Still, she blinked a few times over the discomfort that the abrupt transition from Plato to her present surroundings caused her mind. With some impatience, she trained her eyes on what Rosy was pointing at in the distance.

"Who do you suppose that is?" Rosy asked.

A solitary rider could be seen ambling along on a gray horse at the far end of the very field where the two young ladies had planned to take their morning gallop.

Gussie squinted and put a hand up to shade her eyes against the rising sun pushing its rays through the morning mist, one of the few sunny mornings at this time of year. She soon gave up and shrugged. "I've no notion. It is too bright now. It's a man. That's all I can make out."

Useless information, given that all the fashionable, hunting-mad men of England had retired to the country for the winter sporting season. It could be anyone.

Well, not *anyone*.

Gussie stole a glance to the west, where the smoke from the chimneys of Camrose Hall could be seen rising like gray pencil lines etched into the hazy blue sky of the morning.

He was at Camrose now.

Gussie had been in Rutland for two days and still had not seen a sign of Harry. But he was not just Harry now. He wasn't even Corporal Harry Fletcher anymore. He was Sir Harry Fletcher. An occurrence that no one had thought within the realm of possibility.

"He's going the other way," Rosy said. "Likely he won't bother us. Come. A shilling says Silvertail and I best you today."

Gussie smiled at her friend's enthusiasm that even three years at boarding school hadn't been able to squash. They came up to the opening in the brush barrier separating the lane from one of Squire Barrett's fields and made their way to the top of the field, now barren of any harvest. Any further curiosity about the location of the other rider never entered Gussie's head. If he was going the other way, there was no reason to give it another thought.

The horses, knowing what would happen soon, began jigging at their bits. Although perfectly well-behaved, both Gussie's and Rosy's fathers had made sure their daughters would never be saddled with sluggards and that the girls were expert in handling the added spirit. Their paternal pride would not have been able to bear any kind of missish tepidness when it came to anything equestrian.

Coming to the south end of the field, the ladies positioned their horses side by side. Rosy looked in the stranger's direction again. "He's looking at us. Now he's stopping. Could he be from Oakleigh? Who is staying there with your father?"

"How should I know who my father invited to stay at Oakleigh? Since I knew I was staying with you, I never asked."

Rosy tossed an exasperated look at her. "You say you have a curiosity about everything, but I think you are a curiosity yourself. I'm glad I stopped trying to understand you. Weren't you the *least bit* curious about who might be staying at your own house?"

"It is usually the same lot over and over again, so no. If there was ever anything curious about them, I discovered it long ago. They are not bad men, only boring. Besides, I doubt that rider came all the way from Oakleigh. He doesn't look like my father's cut."

Rosy only hummed in response and went back to the business of their gallop, directing the groom not to follow too closely. "To the tree?" she said.

"To the tree," Gussie confirmed, nodding to the lone little ash tree at the north side of the field.

"Right. On my mark. One, two—oh! Look."

Gussie tightened her grip on the reins and turned her head as her horse, Brutus, strained against this false start. There, toward the east end of the vast field, was the lone rider, holding his prancing horse on the same line as Rosy and Gussie. Having caught their attention, he tipped his head to them and pointed up the field.

"He wants to race," Rosy said, her eyes sparkling. "And look how many mufflers he has on. How funny. You can hardly see his face. Are you ready?"

But Gussie grimaced at this new development. Socializing this early in the morning was not an attractive option. "Oh, Rosy. Let's not—"

"Go!" Rosy yelled, loud enough for the other rider to hear. She put her heel to her horse, and the gelding sprang away like a shot. The other rider followed suit on his gray only a beat after her.

Gussie pressed her lips into a firm line as she held Brutus back an instant before casting her eyes up and giving him his rein. There was nothing for it now. So much for a quiet, intimate morning gallop. Well, if she couldn't have that, at least she could win.

Urging Brutus with her heel and voice, she soon caught up to Rosy, who took the business of a gallop with deadly seriousness. Gussie shot a glance at the other rider and saw him angling across the field, his gray eating up the ground in enormous strides. With the sun behind him growing brighter each moment, she still could not get a good glimpse of him. She only saw the dark mark of a mustache under his nose.

As the horses coursed along the length of the field, the spirit of the competition inched into Gussie's face as she lowered her brows in concentration, a determined grin spreading across her lips. Well behind her, she heard the man let out a laugh followed by the smack of a crop and his deep voice urging more speed out of his mount. There were few horses in the county beyond her father's and Squire Barrett's stables that could outrun Brutus and Silvertail while they carried such light loads as Gussie and Rosy on their backs.

Try as he did, Brutus could not catch Silvertail by the time they passed the tree. Rosy won by half a length. She pulled up immediately and turned back to hail their challenger, but Gussie allowed Brutus to canter a few more strides before falling into a trot, giving him a chance to catch his wind again. Let Rosy, who loved company of any kind, find out who this newcomer was before Gussie, who bemoaned the lack of solitude that was so precious to her each day, had to engage him.

"Did you expect a different outcome, sir?" she heard Rosy say in a good-natured, laughing manner. Though Gussie kept her head down as she turned, she could see that the man had pulled up a few paces away from Rosy. Halfway down the field, the groom could be seen coming along at a brisk trot.

"I confess, I was sure I could beat you," the man replied.

At his voice, Gussie lifted her head and took a good look at him. What was that familiar ring?

He was not looking at Rosy now, but at her, with merry eyes. As her own eyes grew round with disbelief, he continued. "My pride has certainly taken a hit, and I will be more cautious in my challenges the next time around. As it is, care to watch me fish instead?"

The words of one of the many running jokes of her youth made Gussie's mouth drop as wide as her eyes. Rosy let out a cry.

It was *Harry*.

But it wasn't the Harry Fletcher who had run headlong into the army more than four years ago. That Harry had been not exactly stout but soft, with youthful flesh still clinging to him at seventeen and no hint of a beard coming.

The face of the Harry before her displayed a handsome pair of light brown whiskers on either side of his face with a mustache to match. The thicker frame, too used to his mother's sweetmeats, had been replaced by broad shoulders and a firm, sculpted jawline, though his tanned cheeks still held their roundness as he smiled at her.

Gussie only responded by staring all the harder at him. This was *not* her childhood Harry that ran amuck with her and Rosy all over their families' estates, but a man with four years of living in India behind him.

Two weeks ago, he had still been on the other side of the world to her, but the letter arriving from Camrose, *from him*, brought him crashing into her world once more. In all his letters to her telling of the adventures and hard work he had endured while enlisted, she knew he must have changed a little, but the image of her best friend Harry Fletcher had still held fast in her mind all these years. Well, the old Harry may not have survived the harsh Indian sun, but *this* Harry had finally come back to England.

Back home.

Rosy gathered her wits faster than her friend, and while Gussie's mind was still taking in the figure before them, she cried, "Harry! Harry Fletcher, you're finally out among the living! We haven't seen you at all since you've been back." She laughed. "No wonder we bested you. You've never had a proper seat on a horse."

The sound of his name made Gussie give her head a little shake to bring her out of her daze and say in a monotone voice. "Sir Harry. He is Sir Harry now, Rosy."

"Of course," Rosy said. "So much has changed since you've been gone and so have you. What are you doing with such a mustache? Did you join a Hussar regiment?"

At the mention of his new title, Harry ducked his head, one side of his mouth hitched up in what wasn't exactly a smile, but he was quick to retort. "What? Does it not become me? I can tell you I was not the only one with such a face in Bombay."

"It does not," Rosy said bluntly before letting out a trill of laughter at her daring.

Harry only rolled his eyes. He had used that same look so many times when they were young that the motion made him look like the Harry Gussie remembered. Excitement and joy that her dear friend was back welled up in her chest, clearing away the rest of her stupor.

Harry was back.

And so were her questions.

"Harry, where have you been? How long did the voyage take? Were there any typhoons? Did you get to ride an elephant again? Did you ever get to hunt a tiger like you wanted to? The French didn't give you any more trouble, did they? You did not get chosen for the mission to Persia, I remember that. Did you bring a sitar back like you said you would? You must tell me everything. And *why did you not write to me* to tell me you were coming back *before* you left Bombay?"

Chapter Two

Nine-year-old Harry Fletcher bent and stilled in concentration even as the water seeped into his shoes. His mother would scold him for it, but he wouldn't stop. The toad hadn't noticed him yet. Just a few steps closer...

"Are you going to open it up to see what's inside when you catch it? Can I watch?"

Harry jerked his head to the right just enough to see who had asked the question. It was only that skinny little girl from Oakleigh, staring at him with round, curious eyes. His own eyes darted back to the toad, who still rested on the stone, soaking in the afternoon sun, perfectly unaware that it was being stalked.

Anger rose inside him just the same. Couldn't she see that he was in the middle of something important? Why couldn't she go back to the picnic where everyone else was?

Acknowledging her with only a glare, Harry turned back to his hunting. Another careful step...

"Watch out for your shadow."

Harry paused, confused. "What?"

The girl pointed to the ground where his shadow stood in front of his rippling in the gently flowing stream. "It will see your shadow first. Then it will hop away before you can catch it."

Harry looked at her with all the scorn that a boy, and an older boy at that, could muster against a little girl. This particular little girl he'd only seen once or twice last year during his first time staying with his cousin at Camrose. The children of the families of the neighborhood had always been thrown together during picnics, dinners, and the like. The only reason he remembered her at all was because she had never spoken to any of the children when they were together. She'd stayed by her nurse's side and looked at a book of pictures. He didn't know her name, and he had never heard her speak until now.

"I'll catch it my way, thanks," he returned in a loud whisper.

"Your name is Harry. I remember you. You came here last summer with your brother."

When Harry didn't respond, the girl said nothing more. She only watched with a calm, still air that, in truth, was unsettling. Harry bent back to his crouched position and was about to move forward when he noticed that one more step would put his shadow on the rock that the toad was resting on.

Doubt filled his mind. Would the toad really notice? Would it really get scared and hop away before he could grab it? Was she right?

Harry thought he'd better not take any chances. Slowly, he changed his position. The girl cocked her head to one side, watching his progress, but remained silent. Satisfied that he had succeeded in making it look like it was his own idea to approach the toad from a more easterly direction, Harry continued creeping toward it. The girl stepped closer and crouched on the grass near the slope of the bank, eyes intent.

The toad, all the while seemingly unaware of any danger, now twitched. But before it could make its escape, Harry pounced and grabbed it in both hands. The toad squirmed and writhed in Harry's grip, its long back legs sprawling out this way and that as Harry raised his hands up in the air in triumph. "Got it!"

The girl stood up and ran over to him for a closer look. "I didn't think the skin would have so many little bumps. The pictures make it look different."

"What pictures?" Harry asked as he turned the toad up and down and all around, inspecting it.

"In a book my mama showed me. My papa has a big room full of books. We call it the library. Do you have a library?"

"No," he replied, completely disinterested.

The girl stared at him. "You don't? Do you have any books at all?"

Harry shrugged. "We've got some books. Just not a whole room full of 'em. I don't like books anyway. If you're going to keep talking about it, I'm going away."

The girl turned her gaze back to the toad, still struggling against Harry's grip. "What are you going to do to it?"

"Do? Nothing. I only wanted to look at it," Harry screwed up his face. "Why do you want to open it all up? All its guts would come out."

"I saw a dead frog in a glass box at a house once. It had all its guts out next to it."

Harry's interest perked up at that. "Really? What did it look like?"

"It was all dried up and brown and wrinkled. This one looks soft." She lifted a finger as if to touch the toad but hesitated.

"Go on then, if you want. He won't—ugh!"

Warm, wet liquid spread across his palms. Harry dropped the toad and shook his hands furiously. The girl jumped away. "What happened?"

"It—it—" Disgusted and embarrassed, Harry didn't know what to say. "Nothing. I just didn't want to hold it anymore, that's all. It got boring." He wiped his hands on his jacket. "What's your name?"

"Augusta. Mama calls me Gussie."

Harry only hummed in response, not interested in nicknames. He looked back round to where the rest of the boys were playing cricket across the lawn. He couldn't even remember the name of the estate where they were picnicking. The sting of their rejection still smarted. According to them, he would be too small to play for the rest of his life. Well, he didn't want to play with them anyway. He turned back to the girl, Gussie. "Anyhow, care to watch me fish instead?"

***

Harry grinned. There she was. There was the Gussie he knew. For a few moments there, he hadn't known what to make of her staring at him the way she had. He couldn't tell if he had merely surprised her to the point of speechlessness (which was a feat in and of itself) or that she simply did not care that he was back. But the hailstorm of questions with which she now peppered him brought a grin of relief to his face.

She must have only been surprised, just as he had intended when he had the good fortune to catch sight of them during one of his rare rides.

He and Rosy both let her run on until she paused for breath, knowing her so well when she became excited about something. He answered the easier questions first. "The voyage took just over five months; I only succumbed to seasickness rounding the Cape—devilish bad weather there; but I made the acquaintance of a delightful family who boarded in Lisbon, the Fentons. I invited them for Christmas; I rode another two elephants since the first; and I got to carry my commanding officer's guns while *he* bagged the tiger. And I have brought back many more things besides a sitar."

He chose not to answer the last question. The one asking why he had not told her was on his way. Answering that would tip Rosy off to their secret. Indeed, Gussie had said too much already. He hoped that Rosy hadn't picked up on it.

He hoped in vain. Rosy's ears were as sharp as she was hoydenish, and she never liked to be left out of what was going on. "Did you really ride an elephant, Harry? But, how do you know he rode an elephant and didn't go to Pooshra?" she asked, turning to Gussie.

"Persia," Gussie said.

"Persia, yes. How did you know about that?"

Harry cast his eyes back and forth between the girls. What would Rosy think of their secret arrangement if she knew, he wondered.

Gussie set her jaw against her imprudent gaffe but recovered herself in an instant. "Oh, I will tell you later. But Harry, I—I—"

Harry waited. She had lost herself again. This was interesting. There weren't many things that could throw her off balance. He knew she didn't like surprises in general, but he had hoped that he would have been a pleasant one. Perhaps not.

"Did you know that my mother and sisters are at Camrose now?" he asked. "Rosy, I know you've been there with your mother. I'm sorry I couldn't see you then. Too much business."

"Gussie's only just arrived from London," Rosy said. "But two days ago. Did you hear what happened to her sister? Diana had the most delightful adventure!"

"No, I haven't. But you must come visit my mother, with Mrs. Barrett of course, Rosy. And you, Gus, with Diana and Mary?"

"Gussie is staying at Broadstone with me," Rosy said.

Gussie finally found her tongue. "Yes, Diana is in town to be near her...but you do not know it yet. Diana is engaged to be—oh, Rosy, I forget you are here. I shall have to tell you this as well. Diana is to marry the Earl of Sanford."

Rosy's eyes went wide. "Is she already engaged? You told me they only just met."

Gussie pursed her lips and Harry could tell she was inwardly chiding herself. Had he surprised her that much? He could not remember her ever being this careless with things she meant to keep close. Her slightly arched eyebrow gave away her frustration at herself. She still despised feeling flustered, it seemed. She had always looked on it as a weakness, even as a girl.

"They have known each other longer than people have been led to suppose" she said. "But do keep quiet about it. Not a word to anyone."

Rosy nodded her compliance with a somewhat affronted look. She may be a hoyden, but she was as good as her word.

"That is good news," Harry put in. "An earl. Your father must be pleased. And where is Mary?"

"She is with my father at Oakleigh," Gussie replied. "A few of her friends are included in the party my father is hosting."

The groom, all this while waiting some yards away from them, now cleared his throat. "Begging your pardon Miss Barrett, but it's passin' nine o' clock."

"Breakfast," Rosy moaned.

Harry smiled and buried his chin deeper into his muffler. Though he would have loved to speak to them more, especially now that Gussie was talking, he wasn't sorry to end the conversation. He was, quite frankly, freezing. "I won't keep you, then, but do come to Camrose. I'll tell my mother to expect you tomorrow? If that suits."

"Until then," Rosy replied, nodding. "If we must go back now, I am going to have one more gallop. Will you come?"

Gussie shook her head. "No, but wait for me when you get to the lane."

Rosy only nodded before spurring her horse down the field, the groom following.

Gussie turned back to Harry with softened eyes. He knew what she would say next, and the grief that had become his constant companion for nearly a year welled up in his chest.

"I was very sorry to hear about John," she said.

Harry trained his eyes to the pommel of his saddle and nodded his head slowly. "Thank you."

She was still watching him. If she was the same Gussie he had left, a thousand questions would be going through her mind surrounding his brother John's death. She would want to know every detail, as she did with everything else. With any other subject, he would have been happy to oblige, but not with this, and he wasn't sure how to tell her that.

When he looked up, she was still staring at him with those dark, calculating eyes. He prepared himself for the onslaught of uncomfortable curiosity but instead she said, "How is your mother? And your sisters? Have they made Camrose quite their own now?"

A wave of relief came over him, and gratitude, for he could tell she had held back the questions that came so naturally to her. "They are all well. Camrose will never be the same again, I'm afraid."

Gussie smiled. "Good. It was a stuffy place anyway. If there is any hindrance I shall send a note round saying so. Otherwise, Mrs. Fletcher may expect us tomorrow. Thank you, Harry, and welcome back."

Harry tipped his hat to her as she turned her horse and started down the field. She turned her head and threw over her shoulder, "But remember, I am not done with you yet. You still have some explaining to do."

Chapter Three

Having come in from his cold ride only to change and go directly into his study to meet with his steward, Harry stepped down the main staircase of Camrose with heavy, tired footsteps and made his way to the small salon at the back of the main floor of the house.

His mind was in a whirl, full of tenants' names and their needs, rents, farm production, and a host of other things he'd never dreamed he would have to think of. He would take a day of marching in the hot Indian sun over these dismal meetings any time.

His cousin George was supposed to have lived to a ripe old age and have a gaggle of heirs to secure the line of inheritance. Failing that, John should have taken his cousin's place at Camrose and had the same outcome: a score of sons stationed between Harry and the title he did not want. But John had been dead for nearly a year now. The cholera outbreak that had swept through his regiment had been unmerciful to so many.

The only person in the quaint little room in the back of the house was his mother. She sat perched on the edge of a chair and leaned over the little table in the center of the room, scratching some note on a piece of paper. A Norwich shawl in muted hues draped over the shoulders of her gray gown, and a white lace cap adorned her steady brown curls that were only just touched with gray. She said the gray had appeared after the news of John's death.

At his entrance, she looked up and smiled. "The business with Mr. Pritchard is done with, then? And how was your ride?"

"Cold," he replied as he made his way to the fire. He could not decide which side of himself to warm up first. He considered himself a strong man, up for almost anything, but moving from the constant heat and humidity of India to an English winter had become more than just a simple annoyance. He was cold nearly all the time, though it was nothing to the rough, freezing waters and storms around the Cape. Those had nearly done him in.

Mrs. Fletcher chuckled and gave him a look of sympathy. "You will get used to it. But must you be outdoors for so long?"

Harry raised his eyebrows and lips as he turned to face the fire, his backside sufficiently scorched. "Are you waiting for the housekeeper here? You know, the drawing room is better situated for giving your daily orders."

"I gave her my orders already and in this very room. The drawing room is too big and too grand for me just yet. Now, don't frown upon me like that. I know you think I deserve the best, but my mind cannot come round to the fact that I don't live in a little house any longer with barely enough to get by. This room is just the right size for me. You will grow accustomed to the cold, and I will grow accustomed to the house. I've been waiting for you."

"I'm sorry I've kept you. I was late getting back to the house, so Pritchard kept me later than was intended. I came across some friends." He turned and a smile spread across his face as he thought of their faces when they'd realized it had been him. "Gussie and Rosy."

"Augusta Stilwell and Rosy Barrett?" said Mrs. Fletcher. "Rosy was here with her mother, but I have not seen Augusta in ages. I am sending invitations to her family, of course, but I have yet to set eyes on her or her sisters. Was she surprised to see you?"

Harry nodded. "Yes, it was a good joke."

He didn't tell her that Gussie, although surprised at his sudden appearance, had already known he was in England; that writing to her had been one of the first things he had done upon coming to Camrose. His mother might understand but would certainly frown upon the scheme he and Gussie had set up between themselves while he was abroad.

"Is everything ready, then?" he asked.

"Not in the slightest, but we will make do. I—"

A rumbling of running feet above their heads made her cut off her words. Giggles and laughter danced a descant above the pounding footsteps.

Mrs. Fletcher smiled. "There go the girls. They've been exploring again today."

Harry smiled. "They haven't found out every nook and cranny of the house yet? They could not stop talking about it at dinner."

"I thought so, but apparently not. Doubtless they have found a new attic. Are there any secret passages attached to this house? I don't remember anyone mentioning any. We have no ghosts, I know that."

"None that I am aware. If John and I couldn't find any, and believe me, we looked, then the girls couldn't possibly."

At the mention of John, Mrs. Fletcher's eyes dimmed. Something that caught her unawares less frequently nowadays, but it wrung Harry's heart to have caused her pain. He walked over to her and put his arm around her shoulder. "I am sorry, Mama."

Mrs. Fletcher batted his arm away with an impatient hand. "It is so silly of me. He's been gone so long now."

"And you've only known about it for so short a time," Harry murmured, his lips pressed to her lace cap. John had been dead for over ten months, but the letter informing his mother of it had had to cross half the world to tell her the news.

Mrs. Fletcher sniffed and straightened up. "I shall be well, never mind me. Now, do look over this list I've drawn up for the ball. I will not allow you to take any names off, but are there any I've forgotten?"

She picked up the sheet of paper and handed it to Harry, who couldn't restrain his mouth from screwing to one side for a moment. "Ah, yes, the ball."

He schooled his features as quickly as he could, but the slight hesitation in his voice made his mother's eyes widen imploringly. "We shall be out of mourning by then. Dearest, you understand how important it is?"

"Of course I do, love," he said, resting a reassuring hand on her shoulder and lightened his tone. "But couldn't you have chosen a bride for me before I came back from India? Then you wouldn't have to go to the trouble of a whole ball."

She smiled at the joke but only just. "A ball is nothing to choosing a girl for you to marry. There may be many parents who hold to that practice, but we are neither nobility nor royalty. Treaties and wars are not on the line, only your mother's peace of mind."

"And that is worth fighting a war for or breaking a treaty, in my book," Harry replied.

"But it is not so difficult a thing as that, surely?" Mrs. Fletcher said, taking his hand. "You would have married, even while you were in the army, had you found the right girl. I know the circumstances are changed, but—"

Her voice caught and Harry knelt and took her in his arms. "Don't cry, Mama. I know."

She rested her cheek against his shoulder. "I feel that this title, Camrose, and all that comes with it is a curse. No, I didn't mean it to sound so maudlin. But Harry, it has taken two people already. Two robust, strong young men who had no business dying…succumbing to illnesses when there was nothing the matter with them before. And now, you are thrown into this wretched inheritance. Your cousin thought he had all the time in the world to marry. John had no notion it would be his death when he fell ill himself, but he had always been of the same mind. He thought there was time. And, God forgive me, so did I. Such calamities could happen to others, but I never truly believed that they could happen to me or my children until now. Harry, you understand the need. I know it isn't exactly what you should like, but—"

Harry squeezed her tight before bringing her to arm's length. "I will choose a bride at the ball and marry as quickly as possible, Mama. I can't promise I'll wrap myself up in cotton wool for you, but I'll take care of myself. Don't put yourself into such a state." He took her hands and pressed a kiss on each. "Rest easy, Mama. I'll give you a score of grandchildren yet, you see if I don't. Here," he produced his handkerchief and offered it to her. "Dry your eyes and tell me who are your favorite candidates for the position of Lady Fletcher?"

She applied the handkerchief to her nose and suppressed a chuckle. "I will tell you which families are in the country for the hunting season that we will meet with often. Many of them have daughters, but choose your bride for you I will not."

"But you must have some say, of course. I couldn't marry a girl you despise or who doesn't get on with the girls."

Mrs. Fletcher named off the families in their part of Rutland who were staying for the winter and the daughters who were eligible and of an age to think of marriage. Harry recognized many of the names and could even recall some of the daughters of said families.

"Sir Gerald with his daughters, and the squire and his family, of course," Mrs. Fletcher said, ending the list. "Though Rosy hasn't changed much since you've been away. Still as horse-mad as ever, like her father. Her mother is forever lamenting about her sad lack of deportment. If I do hold any influence over you, I shouldn't think she was ready to marry anyone just yet."

"Rosy! No. I can't imagine anyone catching her eye if he didn't have four feet and a tail. Unless that Harrington fellow suddenly appears again. He was the only one I knew of who could turn her head from the stables. That is not likely, though."

"Harrington? Lord Mountbury's son? No, not when his father lost his entire fortune in an idiotic bet," Mrs. Fletcher said, wrinkling her nose in disgust. "I cannot imagine what could possess a man to take such a stupid risk."

Harry gave her a wry look. She would never understand the competitive spirit of some men to win at all costs, especially when the wine and spirits flowed freely.

He had seen plenty of his fellow soldiers fall slave to the insatiable urge, the desperation, to try one more time to see if their luck would turn at the next hand of cards or roll of the dice. He and John had kept an eye out for each other, making sure they never found themselves caught between such unmerciful claws.

He nodded his agreement and went back to the original topic, but not before looking at his left hand and rubbing his thumb over the scar. His thoughts went back to the afternoon under the big birch tree on Broadstone land, trying to escape the heat. He and Gussie had been so bored. Subjects that had never come up between them had risen, and a pact had been made.

Harry's lips twitched at the memory. He remembered the look on Gussie's face this morning when she had finally recognized him. Seeing her brightening eyes and smiling face, a strange sensation had filled him that he could not quite describe. It felt whole, like he was finally home, whatever that meant. "Not Rosy, then. What about...what about Gussie Stilwell?"

"Gussie?"

The surprise in his mother's voice made Harry look up. "If we are to speak of every eligible girl, shouldn't she be included?"

Mrs. Fletcher tilted her head and lowered her brow in thought for some moments, making Harry nervous. At last, she said, "She is *cold*, isn't she? I know you often played together as children, but even then I couldn't see much of anything warm about her. Perhaps it is because she grew up for so many years without a mother, but even before that I could feel that something was not quite right with her. She acted like a little grown woman before she was ten! I always found that unsettling, so unlike my own girls. One can tell she is not fond of others. I don't believe she holds her sisters in any particular affection. I haven't noticed any, even after all these years, have you?"

Harry frowned at this description of his friend. What his mother said raked him the wrong way, but the Gussie he'd known before leaving for the army might be described in that way: cold, and certainly standoffish, especially to strangers.

He remembered his first encounters with her as being excessively awkward and rather annoying, if he were honest with himself. But as they got to know each other, with little Rosy tagging along to complete their set, he had discovered that once Gussie attached herself to someone, she was fiercely loyal to them.

This was confirmed in the lengthy letters she had sent him faithfully over the past four years. He hadn't answered each one, but they'd proven that while Gussie may not be *warm* or affectionate enough to please Mrs. Fletcher's sensibilities, she did not forget her friends. And Harry was one of them.

"I can't say that I agree with you on that head," Harry replied. "She may not be warm, but she does like people."

"And I cannot forget how she treated Amy and Charlotte," his mother continued.

Harry frowned. "What's this? What happened?"

"She didn't make the *least* effort to become friends with them after you left," Mrs. Fletcher said with a lifted brow. "Or beforehand, either. I don't know why, but Amy had her heart set on having Augusta as a friend, but little Miss Stilwell showed no interest whatsoever."

Harry did a few quick calculations in his head. When he had left England, he had only been eighteen and Gussie sixteen, which put his sister Amy down at about twelve. It was not probable that Gussie would have had the patience for a twelve-year-old girl trying to befriend her. Especially if it got in the way of her efforts to learn Greek, which she had been bent on during that time. As far as he could tell from their letters, she was pretty near fluent now.

Mrs. Fletcher continued. "When you left, she rarely came to call, and it always felt like her elder sister had coerced her away from her room full of books. Though I can't say I didn't mind, for my part. All she could talk about was what she had been reading at the time which made absolutely no sense to me. I could not repeat back to you a word she told me on her visits."

"Does she still bury herself in her books? I remember you saying you hoped she would grow out of it." He knew the answer. Her letters to him had been full of the topics which she had been reading in her father's library. But he played ignorant. He could never tell his mother, or anyone for that matter, that he had been writing to a young, unmarried woman across the world for all these years.

Mrs. Fletcher shrugged. "As I said before, I have not seen her in a great while, but I imagine not."

"Well, perhaps you can after tomorrow. I told her and Rosy to bring Mrs. Barrett to you and the girls."

Mrs. Fletcher's face brightened at the mention of her friend. The squire's wife had been something of a mentor to Mrs. Fletcher ever since she'd come to Rutland as a young bride. "Mrs. Barrett? I would love to see more of her now that we are settled and taking calls. But, back to the matter at hand, Harry. I must know, do you really look at Gussie Stilwell as a possible bride?"

Harry balked at the abrupt question, for he did not know the answer. The memory of the pact they had made had never left him after all these years. The scar made sure of that. As he had grown into manhood, he had always been a man of his word. After his father had died, he and John had made a similar pact between themselves (without the blood, for they had outgrown that gruesome practice) to become men who would keep their promises and take care of themselves and their own. But to keep his part of the pact with Gussie, she would have to desire to keep hers, if she remembered it at all.

His mother was waiting for an answer. Harry raised his shoulders. "Only trying to think of everything, so you don't have to," he said with a smile that he hoped was convincing.

It must have been, for she smiled back at him sincerely. "Dear Harry. I will say again, it is your choice when all is said and done. I only ask that you choose someone I can love as a mother as well. But that should be simple, as I find it hard not to love most everyone."

Harry had no time to reply, for just then the door burst open, and his two younger sisters came bounding into the room wearing the most ridiculous hats he had ever seen.

Amy's and Charlotte's heads were engulfed in huge ostrich plumes and broad brimmed hats fitted with luxuriant silks and lace. The things must have been fifty years old, at least.

"Mama, Mama! Look what we found in the attics. There is a whole trunk just full of them!" Charlotte cried as she twirled in front of them. "Harry, don't you think I look extraordinary?"

He laughed, grabbed her about the waist and spun her around several times. "Fit for the queen's drawing room, I'll be bound."

Charlotte giggled and squealed as they spun round and round, her face beaming with pleasure. She had been so young when Harry and John had left for the army, not yet ten years old. Harry could hardly believe his eyes when he saw her again, a blooming young maid of fourteen. She had attached herself immediately to him upon his return, saying it was only because of his regimentals that she had loved him so instantly after such a long time away.

Any mild fondness he felt for his young sisters while in Bombay had increased tenfold at their wholly unrestrained affection toward him upon his return. They cosseted him, ran errands for him with the greatest delight, and generally made much of him, so happy that one of their big, strong brothers had come home at last. He was quite the hero in their eyes with all his tales of the magic and mysteries of India (for he kept all the unseemly bits away from their modest ears). If they kept on as they did, they would make pretty wives for two very fortunate men someday. Whomever his future wife may be, she would be mad not to love his sisters too.

***

After breakfast with Rosy and her parents, Gussie went upstairs to her room, where a great many books and papers awaited to help her pass the rest of the morning in solitude while Rosy went straight back to the stables to visit the broodmares, as was her habit.

Upon entering her room, she did not only find her books waiting for her but Rosy as well. Her friend's narrowed eyes told Gussie that she was in for an interrogation.

"Yes?" she said, trying for a nonchalant attitude.

"Don't 'yes' me in that way, you know why I'm here," Rosy returned. "How did you know so much about Harry when he's been in India all these years?"

Gussie felt her lips tighten only slightly. *Bother.* Though she couldn't have tolerated a dull friend, Rosy was sometimes too clever in all the wrong ways. She sighed and slumped her shoulders slightly, not ready to give up the secret she'd had for so long.

Rosy would never tolerate being kept in the dark if she knew there was something afoot. "Did you get the news from his mother? But I know you haven't visited her much since he went away, you've always been with me. He wouldn't have written to your father, they never got on."

Gussie turned and not only closed the door but locked it as well. "You must give me your word that you will not tell anyone."

Rosy's face brightened, and she went over to the bed and sat down. "I swear on my life I'll not tell a soul."

An exaggerated vow, but acceptable. Gussie gave a farewell glance for the time being to her pile of books and sat on the bed opposite Rosy. "Right. Harry hasn't written to my father. Harry has been writing to me."

The implications of this confession would be obvious to anyone, but as she was talking to a horse-mad girl of nineteen, Gussie waited patiently while Rosy's mind aligned to the proper train of thought.

When it did, her eyes widened, and her mouth opened in shock. "You've been *writing* to each other? You mean you've been engaged to Harry all this time?"

"No, not engaged."

"And without telling me!"

"Hush," Gussie said as Rosy's voice climbed higher and higher. "We are not engaged, but yes, we have been writing to each other."

"But you can't write to each other without being engaged. It would ruin you if you did."

Gussie bristled. "And it is such a foolish thing to be ruined over, writing to a friend who is as unattached to anyone as I am. No, once he told us he was leaving England, I promised myself I wouldn't go on for who knew how long without hearing something of him. We all of us have been friends forever, and to suddenly drop all communication simply because he was halfway round the world and I was a single young lady? No! Besides, to let a chance at a firsthand account of India slip me by while he was there? Again, no!"

"But Gussie, did he write you *back*?" Rosy asked, agog.

"Of course he did," she replied. Her fingers drifted to her dress, and she took a fold of fabric, rubbing it between a finger and thumb.

"Did your father never find out? What about Diana and Mary? They would have noticed a letter from India in the post."

"His letters did not come to the house."

"How, then? I cannot imagine!"

"I'll tell you, but do keep your voice down." Gussie may strain at the social constraints that kept her and the rest of her sex tied down to one path in life, but she knew that if her actions were discovered, life would become very unpleasant for her because of them, and she had no intention of being that uncomfortable just now.

Rosy straightened her shoulders and shifted her position in an apparent attempt to prove to Gussie that she was indeed worthy of such a secret.

Gussie let out a short sigh. Farewell, secret that only she and Harry had shared for so long. "Harry didn't know my plan, but I disguised my writing as a man's and sent him a letter signed 'Gus Stillman' and told him he had better tell me everything he could about India, and that he could direct his letters to the care of a certain place in the city that is occupied by my maid's brother. He is a cobbler and owns a shop in the east end of London. On her half-days, she would visit him, and if there was a letter, she would bring it to me when we were alone."

"She would? My maid would never do that. She is too afraid of Mama to try anything I suggest that may get her cast off."

"I pay her a fee for the extra service and promised her a good reference in case she should get into trouble because of it. And I pay for the letter, of course. Perhaps if I still had a mother like you, it wouldn't have worked. But my new mama certainly does not care what I do, so long as I keep out of her way. All my father cares about is that I ride. When Harry's last letter came from Camrose, Diana and Mary were with me, and so they found out. If Diana hadn't have given up all claim to the household after she came back from New Forest, I would have had a time convincing her to let me keep Alice. But as it was, she only scolded me a little and told me to be more careful."

"'Gus Stillman,'" Rosy said, wrinkling her nose. "Couldn't you have come up with a better name? One that wasn't so close to your own?"

"It worked out perfectly. Harry knew exactly who I was. And who would ever guess? Alice was so discreet up until then."

"Four years of writing to Harry, oh, what adventures he must have told you. Where are the letters? May I see them?"

Gussie shook her head. "I only have the one he sent from Camrose with me. The rest are in a special place back in London. Not even Alice knows where they are."

"Tell me more of them then. What did he do there besides ride an elephant?"

Gussie pressed her lips together. "Are you not usually back in the stables by now?"

"I'm not asking you to talk all day, only a little, please."

So, Gussie gave Rosy a half-hours' worth of news from India, the jungles, the spices, the customs of the people, things that were so strange to two English ladies ("Hindus have to pray *three times a day?*" Rosy cried). Once she was satisfied, she skipped off to the stables and her precious horses and finally left Gussie to bury herself in her books to her heart's content. Gussie did this without giving Harry another thought.

For the most part.

Chapter Four

March 1811,

> *...I had curry for the first time a while back. Have you ever tast-*
> *ed coconut milk? I liked that but the heat of the spices on my*
> *tongue nearly killed me. It is so hot here anyway, why do they*
> *need food like that?*

The next afternoon, the Barrett's carriage rolled up to Camrose bearing Mrs. Barrett, Rosy, and Gussie. Gussie knew Camrose lands almost as well as she knew Oakleigh and Broadstone. She had been to several events and festivities there over the course of her youth, besides walking over in the summers to play with Harry whenever John and Rosy's brothers inevitably cast him out of their play, he being the youngest and therefore least useful in a game of cricket or tug-o-war. That was really the only reason he'd ever consented to play with two girls in the first place.

As the carriage came to a halt, Gussie spied Harry coming out the front door with a smile so big the French could probably see it across the Channel. Gussie did not smile in general unless something truly amused her, but with Harry's grin so infectious, Rosy waving wildly back at him, and the thought that perhaps his smile might actually distract any Frenchman who might happen to see it, the moment became too ridiculous for her not to respond. Harry always had a knack for making her smile for no reason.

Mrs. Barrett, on the other hand, admonished Rosy's energetic greeting while the footman beside Harry opened the door and lowered the step. He then moved aside while Harry stepped up and held out his hand to Mrs. Barrett. "Welcome to Camrose, ma'am. Allow me."

Mrs. Barrett put her slim gloved hand into Harry's large one. Just a glimpse of it told Gussie how strong and steady his grip was, ensuring that Mrs. Barrett had no chance of tripping or falling. But why had Mrs. Barrett's voice become so feathery and flustered all of a sudden?

"Thank you, Sir Harry. You are too kind."

Gussie looked at the woman, instantly curious to discover a reason for this change. Mrs. Barrett, a lady nearer seventy than sixty, was usually quite steady. But good heavens, was she blushing?

She was. Her cheeks were decidedly flushed, and the only reasons for blushing were either she was embarrassed (which couldn't be true, for she hadn't done anything silly), or that she was flustered by Harry's presence, as if she thought he was handsome.

Harry, handsome?

Well, yes, he was. She had noticed it herself yesterday, though she didn't remember blushing about it. Aside from the addition of a mustache, he had always looked that way, he was only more grown now, that was all.

All these thoughts flew through her calculating head as he finished the pleasantries with Mrs. Barrett and turned to help Rosy.

"Rosy," said Mrs. Barrett, "was particularly happy to see you yesterday, weren't you, Rose? Positively could not stop talking about how surprised she was."

Here, Rosy cocked her head and gave a little questioning chirp.

"Was she?" Harry replied. Instead of taking Rosy's outstretched hand, he leaned in, grabbed her by the waist and hoisted her out of the carriage and up over his head before planting her feet on the ground while she let out a delighted laugh. "Rosy! I'd say you're looking well, but you always look better on a horse."

This would be an insult to any lady other than Rosy Barrett. Indeed, Gussie's lips twitched as she saw the shock in Mrs. Barrett's face at Harry's words, but Rosy only laughed the more. "And you look ten times better out of the saddle. Take care no other lady sees you riding, for she'd have nothing to do with you after one glance at your horrid seat."

"Rosy, now really!" Mrs. Barrett said, aghast.

"Sorry, Mama."

But Harry laughed. "Completely deserved, ma'am. She was right to put me in my place."

Gussie, not at all impatient to leave the carriage, watched these interactions with amusement. She loved any chance to watch and study people and would marvel and puzzle over how some people behaved to one person so differently than they would to another. Apparently, the title of baronet did not stop Harry from treating Rosy as he had always done, like the tiresome little sister she had become to him in their youth. And it was clear Rosy loved it as much as if he was just another of her six older brothers, fully bent on teasing her. But she could give a brother back his own, that was clear.

Harry now turned to Gussie. His smile grew, and a certain twinkling light danced in his eyes. Gussie couldn't help smiling back. She hadn't realized just how much she had missed him while he had been so far away.

"Gussie!" he cried, and like Rosy, surrounded her waist with his hands, whose warmth she could feel even through her pelisse. Only he didn't engage in the same theatrics as he had with Rosy. Instead, leaning her forward, he then wrapped his whole arm around her waist and caught her to his chest, twirling round and round while he held her. "How are you, dear friend?" he asked.

The movement fair took Gussie's breath away as her feet swirled about in thin air with her body pressed against Harry's solid torso. A surprised cry squeezed out of her as he twirled her once more before placing her firmly on the ground.

"Harry, you idiot," Gussie said through a laugh and slapped his shoulder before straightening her skewed bonnet.

"Sir Harry, indeed," said Mrs. Barrett, looking flustered at all the sudden activity. "You are not children anymore. Surely a little decorum is in order. You are master of Camrose now, after all."

"Forgive me, ma'am, but I couldn't greet the two of them properly when I caught them riding yesterday," he explained. "I am glad I was able to do so now. I'll behave, Mrs. Barrett, I give you my word, but do come in. My mother and the girls are ready and waiting for you."

He flashed a perfectly magnetizing smile at Mrs. Barrett and she, to Gussie's amused amazement, blushed again. Harry had learned more than just drills in the time he had been away, it seemed. He had always had a winning charm about him, but to master anything takes a good deal of practice.

When Harry's gaze fell on hers for a moment, she arched an eyebrow at him, conveying to him that his charms would not work on her. His lips twisted in what she assumed was an apology.

"And will we have the pleasure of your company too, Sir Harry?" Mrs. Barrett asked.

Harry waved a dismissive hand. "You don't want a great bull calf like me to deal with while you have tea. Besides, I have business to finish before I can allow myself any leisure. Indeed, I only came away from it because I saw I could catch you when your carriage pulled up. But let Nelson here (no relation, I'm afraid) take you to my mother. I'll join you as soon as I can."

He swept his arm in front of him in an invitation for Mrs. Barrett to step up the shallow stone stairs to where the butler had waited for them all this time in stately silence. Once Mrs. Barrett and Rosy passed him, he fell in with Gussie. "I forgot you don't like surprises. Well, no, I didn't forget. I was just happy to see you again. Are you all right?"

Gussie gave him a slightly scolding look. There weren't many people who could get away with such trespasses against her. "Yes, I'm fine. Yes, you're forgiven. And I'm glad to see you too."

***

Harry parted ways with them in the entry hall. The ladies then followed the butler, not to the drawing room, as Gussie had anticipated, but to the back of the house, to a small salon that she had only been in once or twice.

After the butler had announced them and stepped aside, they entered the room and Gussie took stock of her surroundings. Now here was some change. New draperies were attached to the windows, though those could have been changed at any time during the past few years. More potted plants and flowers—those must have been Mrs. Fletcher's own touch, for they were fresh. Mrs. Fletcher always did have a delightful flower garden at their old house, Godfrey Place. On the table in the center of the room was an array of little sandwiches and tarts. Quite a pleasant little room, in fact.

Mrs. Fletcher rose from the settee on which she sat. Her two daughters on the sofa put aside the book of fashion plates they had been perusing. Mrs. Fletcher stepped forward with a smile that was all for Mrs. Barrett, they being great friends. "Anne, my dear, come in. Miss Barrett, Miss Stilwell, welcome."

The cooler tone of voice when Mrs. Fletcher said her name did not escape Gussie. She and Mrs. Fletcher had never gotten on together after Harry left, though she couldn't think of a particular reason or event that was to blame for it. Their natures were simply the opposite of each other.

Still, Gussie, for her sister Diana's sake, never forgot her manners in front of others who were not familiar with her peculiarities (not anymore, anyway), and conducted herself with aplomb while the ladies settled into their seats and Mrs. Fletcher started to pour the tea.

"Thank you," said Mrs. Barrett. "Have you taken many other callers since we've been here last? People must be curious, now that you're all settled in."

"As settled as we shall be, I feel. Though it is all still very strange, isn't it, girls? So unlike what we are used to."

Mrs. Fletcher cast an amused glance at her daughters when she said this. Amy and Charlotte began at once telling of the things they had discovered while exploring the house, and only an admonishment from their mother kept them from running out of the room to bring back some old hats and feathers to display to their visitors.

Gussie could feel her chest tighten against their actions. There was a lot of finishing to be done with them before they could go out much in society. Their loud, high voices and quick movements unsettled her and always had. And the way they sat side by side, shoulders touching, was a curious thing to watch. Gussie's own flesh shivered against the idea of the continuous touch against her shoulder were she in a similar position. Who would want to be so close to anyone for so long? How peculiar.

Harry's name being said by Mrs. Barrett pulled Gussie out of these thoughts, and she turned her attention back to what the two older ladies were saying.

"Yes, my son has been a great help to me and the girls, of course. He has taken all this on as best as anyone could," said Mrs. Fletcher.

"Sir Harry," Mrs. Barrett said, allowing the title to float in the air for them all to inspect. "It is never what one would have thought to happen, my dear Maria. Do you still plan to host a ball in six weeks' time for...?"

She raised her eyebrows meaningfully, leaving Rosy and Gussie to stare at her, waiting for the rest.

But Mrs. Fletcher seemed to know what she was implying. "Yes, And for that precise purpose."

If the two mothers thought they were being discreet about the subject, they failed. Mrs. Fletcher wanted Harry to get married and was holding a ball to help push things along. Gussie had figured that out as soon as Rosy told her there was going to be a ball at Camrose.

One of Gussie's peculiarities was to be able to see into the future of possibilities by asking several simple "what if this should happen" sorts of questions. While the idea that Mrs. Fletcher should wish for a daughter-in-law wasn't an unexpected thunderbolt upon Gussie's equilibrium, somehow hearing the implications out loud that Harry would be getting married sometime in the future rattled her. Of course Harry must marry, but she did not like it at all, and nothing in his letters told her that he would like it either, poor fellow.

But that wouldn't happen for some time. Harry had only just returned to England and was but twenty-two years old. In Gussie's mind, the correct order of things would be for Harry to spend a few years concentrating on the Camrose estate he had inherited, then think of marriage when he was older.

But what about the Pact?

Mrs. Barrett nodded at Mrs. Fletcher's words, apparently much less affected by them. "I wish you all speed in that endeavor and that he may find someone within our little community to suit the purpose—"

Gussie was hard put not to cast her eyes up to the ceiling in frustrated disgust. *To suit the purpose*, as if marrying Harry was a position to be filled by a series of interviews and presented references. She may not hold marriage up as a thing to be desired, but if Harry was being forced into the institution, he would at least want someone who would do more than just 'suit the purpose.'

"It is a shame that he may not go up to London in the spring, when the season would bring everyone together instead of being scattered about the country," Mrs. Barrett went on, "but if I may say, though we are small, Rutland is home to some of the best company."

Here she smiled proudly and turned her head to her daughter who, by the look of it, had completely lost interest in the conversation and was methodically chewing her sandwich while staring out the window into the garden. If Gussie knew anything about her, Rosy was probably imagining herself jumping a magnificent horse over every little bush and shrub she saw to pass the time until they left.

Mrs. Barrett must have thought something similar, for she pursed her lips and shot out an impatient hand to tap her daughter's shoulder. Rosy jumped and came out of her daze with a look of innocent inquiry.

Gussie held back a chuckle as she realized what was afoot in Mrs. Barrett's head, but only just. If Mrs. Barrett thought Rosy would do for Harry, Rosy would have something to say about that.

Though she did her best to hold back, she did make enough of a sound for Mrs. Fletcher's eyes to come round to her. "And you, Miss Stilwell, how does your family? Are not your sisters here? I did not see them at church with your father."

Mary had been there, plain as day. Everyone seemed to forget about Mary. Gussie explained her family's whereabouts for the winter. Diana had stayed in London not only to help their new mama-in-law, Phyllis, recover from giving birth to a healthy, squalling boy, but to be near her intended. Sir Gerald, while over the moon about finally producing an heir, had not let the event get in the way of his customary plans to hunt the whole winter long. He had broken up the household mere days after Phyllis had passed through the ordeal safely.

"It has reached my ears," said Mrs. Barrett, "that Diana is being courted by none other than the Earl of Sanford."

News traveled fast. Gussie looked at Mrs. Fletcher to gauge her reaction. The earl's past reputation was not one that ladies could discuss over tea and cakes.

Mrs. Fletcher opened her eyes. "An earl! Well, that is something, to be sure. Though Diana is so beautiful, it is no wonder. But so soon after her ordeal in Hampshire!"

Her response satisfied Gussie that Mrs. Fletcher had only heard what Diana and Hugh had meant for her and the rest of the world to hear: that while riding in New Forest, Diana had taken a fall and had been cared for by an old farmer and his wife while she recovered, and that she and the earl had arrived in London at the same time quite by coincidence. So far, no one had suspected that it had been Hugh who had rescued her and brought her to his own hunting lodge to recover. He had followed her up to London when he'd realized he didn't want to live without her, and Diana was of quite the same mind.

The topic then switched to Diana's prospects of receiving an offer and how soon that might occur, which was a relief to Gussie. She had loved Diana forever and liked Hugh more and more each day. She could picture them marrying with little effort, and much happiness.

She had lost track of what was being said, but Mrs. Barrett's words addressed to her brought her back from her thoughts. "With your sister well on her way to matrimony, it will be your turn next, Gussie."

Gussie blinked and replied just as the door to the little room opened to admit someone. She did not look to see who. "Oh, I shall never marry. I should not enjoy it, and it would not suit me at all, I'm sure."

Chapter Five

October 1811

...I wish you could have seen the look on our cook's face when I told her to find a recipe for curry. I do believe she thinks she may be thrust down to hell if she made a dish from such a wild, heathen place. I wonder what stories have been told to her. Everything you have described so far has made me long to make the journey...

"It would not suit me at all, I'm sure."

Those were the words which Harry heard when he entered the room. They made his step falter slightly.

He shouldn't have been surprised, he supposed. Once Gussie's mind was made up, it was made up. She had been so bent on staying single since she was a child—a child who'd thought she had the world figured out by the time she was thirteen. But to hear the flat determination in her voice stung him a little.

That odd feeling of wholeness, of *home* that had cropped up when he had seen her in the field had stayed with him through the day before and into this morning, growing stronger when he had greeted her at the carriage.

It was not unlike the calmness he'd had when rereading her letters after John's death. He had been desperate for anything to take his mind off his loss. When he had done all that his commanding officers would throw at him, he found himself going to Gussie's letters. In them, she knew nothing about John and so she could help him escape his grief for a time with her no-nonsense accounts of home and the questions she had of India.

The ladies looked up at his entrance and welcomed him. Amy and Charlotte eagerly invited him to sit next them and lost no time in making up a plate and cup of tea for him.

"Forgive the intrusion," he said by way of greeting, "but the thought of old friends and lovely neighbors in the house, well, it was too tempting to pass up."

Mrs. Barrett beamed at the compliment. "Oh fie, Sir Harry. As if we are anything special. Maria, did he tell you of the surprise he gave Rosy in the field yesterday?"

Harry grinned at Rosy and Gussie as he took his seat between his sisters. "Yes, we had a run in."

Gussie looked at him with a small, familiar smile. "You were bundled up as if you were bound for the top of the world. We haven't even had the first snow yet."

Harry raised a brow at her. "Give it time. I shall get used to it."

He felt the air tense up around his mother. "Yes, indeed, Miss Stilwell. He shall. Anne, do you know that Amy has been trying her hand at the harp in the drawing room every day, haven't you, dearest? We've never had an opportunity to learn, and she simply can't wait until I take her to London to the masters to teach her." She turned to Amy. "When we are finished, do let us go into the drawing room and you can show us what you've taught yourself, can't you, my love?"

Amy nodded enthusiastically. She was never one to pass up a chance to be the center of attention, even if her playing had yet to produce anything beyond a simple tune plucked out one string at a time. But the abrupt change of subject that Mrs. Fletcher introduced only further confirmed to Harry that his mother wasn't fond of Gussie.

Rosy spoke up. "The harp? Why, Gussie—"

Gussie set a firm hand on top of her friend's lap. "Gussie *loves* to hear the harp played. How splendid."

Harry blinked and looked from Gussie to Rosy. What had Rosy been about to say that Gussie had put a stop to?

"Wonderful," Mrs. Barrett said to fill in the awkward moment that had come over the party. "I should love to hear Miss Fletcher play too. Perhaps she could play at the ball next week? You are going to the Welbeck's party, Maria, are you not? They are calling it a ball, but it is quite an informal thing."

At this Amy shook her head wildly, and Harry laughed, as did everyone else in the room except Gussie. Amy may love being the center of attention, but only on her own terms.

"Yes, we are going," Mrs. Fletcher answered. "I shall depend greatly upon you, Anne, to help me through the ordeal of my first party as the mother of a baronet."

"Tush!" Mrs. Barrett replied. "You were the wife of a gentleman before this. It will be nothing."

Harry's lips tightened. Yes, the wife of a gentleman who couldn't keep his finances in good enough order to leave much for his family to live on after his death. Finding out how bad matters were after the burial, Harry and John had packed off to the army so Mrs. Fletcher could use what little they had left on the girls. His eyes darted to Gussie and saw her looking back at him, sending him a quick, wry twist of her lips. She remembered what he thought of his father. She had been a listening ear to his complaints on more than one occasion before he sailed away.

"It isn't as if you will not know anyone there," Mrs. Barrett continued. "Our families have been here for I don't know how long. We have all known each other forever, and we won't stop liking you any less simply because Sir Harry has inherited Camrose. Do not put yourself into a fret, my dear."

Mrs. Fletcher smiled back at her friend and held her hand out to Harry, who took it and squeezed it in support of her. "Thank you," she said. "It is just all so strange. To be in this big house not just for a visit, but to stay. And for Harry to take on the estate and all the responsibilities that entails...but we shall grow accustomed to it, won't we Harry? Girls, shall we?"

The party rose and made their way to the door. Harry fell in behind Gussie, and as they moved along, his eye caught her fingers pinching a fold of her pelisse and rubbing it between them. She had done that when she was a child when she was nervous.

He stepped up close behind her. "You're going to the Welbeck's next week, aren't you? I'm rather counting on it."

She craned her neck to look back at him and stopped until they were abreast of each other. "Yes, I am."

"Mama tells me there will be dancing, musicians, and everything. Will you dance the first two with me, then? Are you engaged for them already?" Gussie raised a brow at him, which made him smile. "What?" he asked. "Are you still as fond of dancing as you *weren't* in your letters?"

Her eyes darted toward the rest of the company at his words. "Hush. And yes. On both counts. I am not fond of it, but I will dance with you, if you wish."

If he wished it? What if he wanted her to wish for it as well? Sudden annoyance sparked up in him. It was like she was doing him a favor, but for herself, she could do with or without him. "What a sacrifice. You are very good. I'm much obliged."

He didn't mean for his words to sound so curt, but they must have had a great deal of sharpness in them for the way Gussie opened her eyes at him. He stepped ahead of her to tweak one of Charlotte's curls, making her turn her head and laugh at him. His mother's words came back to him about how cold she thought Gussie could be. She certainly answered questions honestly. He had, after all, asked if she still didn't like dancing. Now, annoyance at the thought that he quite possibly had set himself up for such an answer flitted through his mind. But by this time, they were in the drawing room.

Mrs. Fletcher swished her hands at the harp, encouraging Amy forward. She skipped up to the instrument and sat down on the stool behind it, situating herself and the harp to her liking.

"Go on, my love," Mrs. Fletcher said, "and play for us that quaint little tune you picked up so quickly, and all on your own."

***

Mrs. Fletcher's maternal pride positively overwhelmed the room as they all listened to Amy pluck out Greensleeves with one finger.

Gussie turned a discreet look at Rosy and Mrs. Barrett. Rosy's face told her she was listening politely, but this may have only been because her mother was sitting next to her and she didn't fancy the scold she would receive afterward if she became inattentive. Perhaps she was now imagining that it was a horse playing the harp with its lips instead of Amy.

Mrs. Barrett had a fond light in her eye as she watched Amy continue to pluck away. Gussie turned her attention back to the performer. It was clear that she had had no instruction whatsoever on the harp. Whoever taught her would have to correct her form.

Amy plucked the last string with an exaggerated flourish and looked at the company with a smile that told Gussie she expected a standing ovation.

She nearly got it. The two mothers and Charlotte clapped with the enthusiasm that a whole orchestra would be satisfied with. Gussie politely tapped her hands together as she watched everyone else in the room.

She was hesitant to look at Harry. If she'd known that saying she would dance with him after he asked her would put him out, she wouldn't have done so. But when she finally looked his way, she found him looking right back at her. It must have taken her heart by surprise, for it skipped a beat. She turned her eyes back to the harp, not liking the feeling. What had happened? He hadn't snuck up on her, so it wasn't fear or surprise. But what else could it be?

The sound of her name coming from a vague voice outside her thoughts caused her to answer while only half attending. "Yes, I should think so," she replied.

Realizing that she had no idea what she was answering to, she gave herself a small start to shake her back to reality. "Forgive me, what was that?"

Mrs. Barrett spoke again. "I said we should be happy to come over to help write out the invitations to the Fletcher's ball and told Mrs. Fletcher what a pretty hand you have in particular, Gussie, dear."

Gussie's face stiffened but she said nothing to contradict Mrs. Barrett's words. In the words of Harry, written in several of his letters (though she was certain he'd used a stronger word when he was with his brothers in arms), *blast* her wandering mind! But there was nothing for it. She had agreed to it already, and it would be bad form to go back on it now.

Thankfully, Mrs. Barrett and Mrs. Fletcher looked to be saying their farewells. Gussie and Rosy began drawing on their gloves and were soon being escorted by Harry back out to the carriage.

"Now, Sir Harry, I hope you do not feel the need to lift any of us *into* the carriage," Mrs. Barrett said with a teasing grin.

"Not at all, ma'am. I am on my best behavior now, I promise," returned Harry as he handed her up the step. He took Rosy's hand next, their exchange of silly faces going unnoticed by Mrs. Barrett.

He put his hand out to Gussie. "Will you be at the hunt tomorrow?"

"Yes. My father expects it."

"Until tomorrow, then. And do be sure to practice your steps this week so you don't crush my poor toes."

Relieved that he didn't seem to be angry with her anymore, Gussie threw a withering smirk at him. "A pleasure, as always, *Sir Harry.*"

He laughed at her exaggerated tone and handed her up into the carriage. As he let go, she felt his thumb linger and brush slowly against her gloved hand. The tingling sensation left behind stayed with her while the footman lifted the step and shut the door. Indeed, it not only stayed, but seemed to travel up her arm, only fading once it reached the top of her head.

Harry stayed to watch the carriage roll away from the house, giving a final wave of his hand, which all the ladies returned before settling back into their seats.

"Well!" Mrs. Barrett said. "He is something, isn't he? Quite grown up now, and handsome too. Though I cannot like the whiskers. Don't you think he's handsome, Rose?"

Rosy put this question to thought before giving a little shrug. "I didn't really notice. He's Harry, that's all. I do like the mustache."

Mrs. Barrett lifted a brow, impatient with her daughter's answer. "He is *quite* handsome, and now the master of Camrose! With my dear Maria here as well. I think we shall be visiting often. There shall be plenty of opportunity for you and Harry to become reacquainted. You as well, Gussie. And Rose, I wish you to be very attentive to him."

Rosy scrunched up one side of her face. "To Harry? Good heavens, why?"

Gussie suppressed a knowing smile and tried to picture the end result that Mrs. Barrett had undoubtedly been imagining for some time. Harry and Rosy coming together in marriage? It could be possible. They liked each other well enough. Perhaps they could have a successful union if Harry did not stand in the way to the stables and the two of them could refrain from teasing each other to death.

Gussie's lips twitched. Perhaps not. Rosy, the tail end of six older brothers, probably saw Harry as merely an additional sibling to irritate, and he'd certainly acted like one when they were children. If Mrs. Barrett had any hopes of matrimony in that direction, Rosy and Harry would have to change a great deal.

Mrs. Barrett answered Rosy's blunt response with some sharpness. "Because he has only just returned to England and is doubtless in need of some friendship while he settles his family at Camrose, that is why. It is a great thing, inheriting an estate and all that goes with it. I simply ask that you be attentive to him."

"We are already friends," Rosy replied.

"A friend does not say such cutting things as you did when Sir Harry greeted us today."

Rosy shrugged her shoulders and looked out the window with maddening nonchalance. "This one does. That's how we've always been. We like it. He hasn't changed a bit, don't you think, Gussie?"

But to this Gussie could not agree less. Harry was still Harry, through and through, but she was not blind to the maturity that four years abroad had given him, not only in his looks, but the way he carried himself. There was a certain self-assurance about him now that had been absent before the army. And Gussie had to agree with Mrs. Barrett. Harry was handsome. He had always been a good-looking boy but now, as a man...

Mrs. Barrett cut in on Gussie's musings before she could answer her friend. "It is not becoming in a young lady, and I would have you stop such childish behavior to each other this instant. That is not how one treats a man of property and position. And stop shrugging. It is extremely vulgar. Suppose he should ask you to dance at the Welbeck's next week?"

"I'll dance with him, and gladly."

This was too true but would not in itself do anything to promote the feelings that Mrs. Barrett seemed bent on producing between the two young people. Rosy loved a dance and would happily accept anyone who asked her. But here in the carriage, it was clear from her furrowed brow that she did not realize yet just where her mother's thoughts lay.

Rosy continued. "But I don't treat everyone this way, Mama, you know that. This is Harry. This is why we are friends. We like to tease each other, to see who can best the other."

"And it stops now, do you understand me?" Mrs. Barrett said in a voice that told the two girls that there was an end to it.

"Yes, Mama," Rosy replied with a detached sigh. Gussie's heart went out to her friend. Rosy and her mother were at odds more often than not. It had ever been so.

Her own mother, Lady Stilwell, had never been so strict, but then, Gussie had only been twelve when she died. None of the Stilwell girls were yet of marriageable age when she had passed away. Perhaps finding a match for a daughter was a greater burden to mothers than Gussie realized. Her father's wife, Phyllis, had certainly thrown broad hints to both herself and Diana that the sooner they married, the happier everyone would be— most of all, Phyllis.

Rosy set her elbow on the edge of the carriage door and propped her cheek against her fist. With her jaw slightly jutting out and her eyes staring blankly out the window, Gussie knew she had retired into the sulks and really couldn't blame her. She tried to think of a distracting subject to take Mrs. Barrett's attention away from her daughter.

"That's better," Mrs. Barrett said. "You are all of you grown up now, and it is only right that we behave so. I wish you to be attentive to him, that is all. Now, we shall all have a grand time at the Welbeck's, shall we? Suppose Sir Harry asks you for the first two dances, Rose, wouldn't that be a treat?"

"He already asked Gussie for them. I heard them in the hall."

Rosy's answer, given so bluntly, nonplussed her mother considerably, for her eyes widened and she was speechless for some moments, looking from Gussie to Rosy a few times. "Ah. I see. Well, what a treat for you then, my dear, to be able to dance with someone who has always been such a friend."

Chapter Six

"'I wish you to be attentive to him, that's all.' Attentive. What does that even mean?"

Up in her bedchamber, Gussie watched Rosy, red-eyed and sniffly, pace about the room while she recovered from the confrontation with her mother in the carriage. On the last word, she threw the shawl she had been wringing between her hands to the floor. "Can't she just leave me alone? There was nothing wrong with how I treated Harry, was there? We've always been like that."

"Nothing wrong if you remain friends," Gussie said from her chair. She looked at Rosy, still moving like a keyed-up filly, and let out a sigh. "Do you want to know what she's thinking? I'll tell you, but you won't like it."

Rosy stopped pacing. "Really? Try me."

Gussie raised her eyebrows, displaying her disbelief.

It worked.

Rosy placed her hands on her hips. "Come now. Let's have it."

Rosy never backed down from an unknown challenge once her courage was put into question. Gussie softened her expression. "Your mother wishes you to pay attention to Harry in the hopes that he will like you enough to offer for you."

Shock settled onto Rosy's face as she registered Gussie's words. And if Gussie knew her friend at all, the next expression would be one of...yes, there it was...

Rosy nearly howled with laughter, doubling over, and clutching her sides. "Marry Harry? *Harry?* Oh, that is too—how could she possibly—what must she be *thinking?*"

While Gussie could appreciate Rosy's antics, a weight seemed to lift off her shoulders. A weight she hadn't realized had been there until it went away. A small part of her (a tiny part, really) had been worried that Rosy just might take to the notion of viewing Harry as a potential husband. She let out her breath in a rush. How long had she been holding it?

"It is perfectly reasonable for her to think it. Now that he has come into property he must marry. Doubtless she thinks that since you have been friends your whole lives, you will have an advantage over any other candidates for the position."

"But he's like a brother to me!" Rosy said, wiping her eyes. "That is too rich. If anything, *you* should marry Harry. He's always liked you best."

It was Gussie's turn to be surprised. "Me? What makes you say that?"

Rosy picked up the shawl from the floor and began swinging it to and fro. "It was obvious that it was you he wanted to play with, in the beginning, anyway. He only tolerated me because you made him—I was so much smaller. But could you imagine being married to him? I'm sure I could not."

Married to Harry. Ever since his letter informing her that he had inherited Camrose, the pact had never left Gussie's thoughts. She could concentrate on plenty of other things as it did not distract from her everyday routines, but it was there, patiently sitting in its designated corner of her mind waiting until she decided what to do with it. All this time, she had never sat down and really thought about what the pact, if upheld by both parties, would mean. She would be married to Harry. Living with him, raising his children.

Children.

The thought made Gussie's stomach twist with nerves. If she had children, that would mean she would have to carry them and bear them, which just the thought of had kept her up many a night.

She had seen horses bear their foals. Rosy had witnessed several births and snuck Gussie into the barn once. Watching the mare with her enormous belly, glistening with sweat, pacing up and down the length of the loose box, lying down several times only to get back up and start pacing again until finally staying down and straining so. The first experience of this part of creation had made Gussie nauseous, but her curiosity kept her there until the mare was licking clean a brand-new foal, whispering soft nickers to it as if the pain she'd had to go through beforehand was nothing, but Gussie could not get the picture of the travail out of her mind. It frightened her. Such discomfort! Such pain!

"Shouldn't that kill them?" Gussie had asked Rosy afterward.

"It does, sometimes. I've never seen it, but I cried and cried when Papa told me we lost a mare that way once," Rosy replied, completely unaware of the horror her words had struck into her friend's bosom.

Having babies could *kill*?

The women surrounding her in her life did not talk about such things in relation to themselves, and Gussie had learned the hard way that they did not like being asked about it point blank. Would they get any bigger? How did it feel when the infant moved? Was it uncomfortable? And, most importantly, how in the world did they allow themselves to get that way?

The last question had gotten her a tremendous scold from her mother when she was naught but seven years old. Gussie had seriously embarrassed the lady whom they were visiting with her outrageous question, and the subject was forbidden from that time forth. But after Lady Stilwell's death, with her freedom in the library and her questions to the servants over the years (they would talk about so many things that the ton would not, for a few extra shillings), Gussie had discovered just what had to happen for the creation of life to come to pass.

That enlightenment had been startling, to say the least. It made the whole idea of marriage all the more distasteful.

She still hadn't responded to Rosy. Pushing aside these anxious thoughts, and Harry with them, Gussie said, "What a thing, to be sure. But don't worry, I am sure your mother and father would not force you into something you were so opposed to. Once she sees that you have no interest, your mother won't press you so. You're still a bit young to think of marriage."

"I'm nineteen. Mama was seventeen when she married Papa," Rosy replied. "I hope she realizes that Harry and I would never do for each other soon. But," she paused as a new thought struck her mind. "What if Harry falls in love with *me*?" She went over and knelt in front of Gussie. "Let's you and I make a vow, here and now, that we shall never do anything to make him fall in love with either of us."

Gussie huffed out a laugh. "I do not make vows. Especially ones as silly as that." She had learned her lesson!

Vows and pacts may seem like a good idea in an impetuous moment, but they could cause the parties privy to it serious discomfort if they ever came to pass. Gussie felt it, anyway. She had yet to discern if Harry felt the same way or even remembered what they had promised all those years ago. But from a very young age, Gussie had felt a keen duty to keep any promise she made. The only reason she'd made the Pact with Harry was her assurance that Harry's inheriting Camrose would be utterly impossible.

Well, here they were with Harry now—*Sir* Harry! She would never be so taken in again.

She took Rosy's hand in a firm grip. "I see nothing in Harry's actions toward you to make me think he might want you for anything other than a little sister to pester and annoy, since his own sisters are too sweet to give him back his own. So, never mind what your mother thinks. She shall soon see that the two of you wouldn't suit. Calm yourself. Do you need to go and groom Silvertail to make you feel better?"

Rosy sighed. "No. Though I might anyway. That sounds like just the thing to do until dinner. I will."

With a smile and a firm nod of her head, she let go of Gussie's hands and walked to the door. Before she opened it, she turned around, a scowl on her face. "Did you suggest that only because you're really worried about me, or because you really just want to shut yourself up in here and read for the rest of the afternoon?"

"Yes," Gussie replied with complete sangfroid until a mischievous smile escaped.

Mock outrage crossed Rosy's face, and she stuck her tongue out at Gussie before leaving the room.

Once alone, Gussie took up her book on Mr. Keyssler's European travels from sixty years ago. But instead of opening it, she fiddled with the edge of the pages, running her finger from the last page all the way to the first. How to bring up the Pact with Harry? Should she bring it up at all? Did he even remember it? And if he did, why hadn't *he* brought it up yet? *Harry, do you remember that time when we arranged our own marriage under the preposterous circumstances of your cousin's father, your cousin* and *your own brother all having to* die *before we would marry each other? Well, here we are...*

Gussie swallowed an uncomfortable lump in her throat and pressed a hand to her mouth. When she looked at the Pact from that angle, she felt like a cold-blooded monster. What had she been thinking as a child? And Harry to agree to it! How gruesome. But it had been so outrageous in the first place, the thought of Harry coming into Camrose when there were two heirs before him. Their cousin George had inherited some six years ago, after the death of his father. And now, to think that he *and* John Fletcher, both in the prime of life, had fallen within months of each other...

She couldn't be the one to bring it up. She wouldn't. It was too awful a thing, and to make Harry talk about it when his life must be all in a tumult was a selfish thing to do.

No, if he had forgotten, let him forget. If he wanted to talk about it, let him bring the matter to her. She knew that if left unresolved, the Pact would likely haunt her well-ordered mind for some time. But she would take that discomfort and gladly since Harry had so much of his own already.

Chapter Seven

May 8, 1812

The cassia trees are in bloom. Do you have a book describing those? Massive fountains of yellow flowers hanging down from the branches that look like gold. Even the incandescent orange glow of a sunset can't take away from their radiance. Well! That last phrase was poetic, wasn't it? Do you think I went into the wrong profession?

The next morning saw Harry mounted on his gray gelding surrounded by several members of the neighboring gentry and a pack of noisy, smelly hounds eager to begin the hunt.

Mr. Sydney of nearby Lilford Hall had planned a whole morning full of hunting and shooting followed by luncheon. Several footmen, some from the house, some brought by their masters to help, walked around from horse to horse, offering mugs of ale while trying to avoid tripping over the dogs. Squire Barrett, Rosy's father and the master of hounds, kept them pretty well in hand, but there had already been one footman fall flat on his face.

The other men joining the hunt, including Gussie's father, Sir Gerald, couldn't have been more agreeable and welcoming to Harry, in their manly way. This was not surprising, for Harry could get on with anyone, really. He loved company. His broad, attractive smile and an eagerness to enjoy himself wherever he was made it easy for others to like him. It was a rare thing that he didn't get on with someone, and today was no exception.

He kept the men laughing with his jokes and observations, knowing full well that they would likely be laughing *at* him before the day was over. He had never been much for riding, to say nothing of hunting, and he was sure he would be the butt of several jokes. But he could take it in good part.

There were few women present, it was so early, and only one on horseback, an upright, regal-looking blonde with a light in her eye that told everyone that she knew just how magnificent she looked in her deep blue riding habit, her hat tipped at a mischievous angle. Harry recognized her but could not place a finger on her name, though had caught her looking in his direction more than once. So far, none of the men had offered to introduce him.

More ladies would come, as the morning went on, to spend the day at Lilford until luncheon. Harry knew Rosy would likely come to see the men off, but would Gussie come with her or choose to come when the day was more advanced? He wanted, well, *needed* to talk to her about the Pact, if she remembered it at all...ah, there they were.

Rosy and Gussie, with a groom in tow, appeared trotting down the drive coming around some shrubbery and were soon being hailed by the rest of the party.

Rosy joined the men with every expectation of a warm welcome, and she got it. It seemed all the men, the older ones, at any rate, simply doted on her and spoke with her in such a way that Harry, as Gussie rode up to him, asked, "Is Rosy riding the hunt as well?"

"Oh, yes. She never misses a hunt."

"Really? I've never seen a woman on the hunt before. Not that I've been to many myself. Certainly not in India."

Gussie's lips curved up, but only a little. "But Rutland and Bombay are so different, geographically. I don't imagine there are many places for a gallop amid the jungles."

"Thick, humid, and hot forests. There are a lot of them. There are open places too, though we are rather short on proper English foxes, funnily enough. The monkeys are too fast, the elephants too boring, and if you start chasing a tiger on horseback, well, they usually have something to say about that. Very stuffy opinions about being chased, tigers have. And don't even mention the cobras. They're churlish no matter what you do."

Harry watched with satisfaction as Gussie held back a laugh at his ridiculousness. It felt so good to make people laugh. Laughing people meant happy people, and Harry loved being happy. To get even a smile out of Gussie had always been an objective with him when they were young. She had always been so serious, even when any of his many hare-brained adventures had gone awry. Rosy would double over laughing when he lost his balance on a log and fell into the lake or got bucked off by a pony who had had quite enough of the heavy-handed mauling of its mouth. But Gussie would only lift her eyebrows and shake her head in a way that said *I told you so* before helping him up.

Now, as they waited for Squire Barrett to start the hunt, she looked at him with the smile still intact. "I'm sure the foxes here have their own opinions on being chased—"

Here she was interrupted by the blonde in the blue habit who came up on Gussie's right. "Augusta Stilwell, it has been quite some time since I have had the pleasure. Are you well?"

While her words were directed at Gussie, her eyes frequently darted to Harry's. Gussie's smile vanished, but she nodded her head to the other girl. "Amelia."

Amelia, that was her name. Amelia Blackwell. Her father's estate lay a few miles from Camrose, with the village of Ryhall between them. He hadn't had much to do with that family, but he could never recall seeing any of the Blackwell children looking anything but perfect as they sat in their pew at church.

Amelia waited for Gussie to say more but several seconds went by in awkward silence. The air of dislike coming off Gussie was palpable, and Harry wondered what kind of story was behind the two of them. Amelia finally looked at him and spoke. "You are new to our community, I think. Though you seem to know Miss Stilwell. Won't you introduce me, Augusta?"

Gussie looked as if she was about to give a firm 'no' to Amelia's request, but Harry kicked her boot with his own, calling her to order.

She eyed him but relented. "Sir Harry Fletcher, may I introduce Miss Blackwell. Miss Blackwell, Sir Harry Fletcher of Camrose."

Amelia leaned over and reached a white gloved hand across Gussie. "A pleasure, I am sure, Sir Harry. Miss Stilwell and I were at school together, weren't we, Augusta?"

Harry took her hand and nodded over it—but only just—before letting go. The way Gussie's back had straightened and her shoulders stiffened, he could tell she did not like the intrusion on her space, and he rather agreed with her. But perhaps Miss Blackwell did not know Gussie didn't like quick movements too close to her.

"Pleasure's all mine, I'm sure," he replied.

"I have heard that you've come all the way from the East Indies. But tell me, from where did you come before you joined the army?"

Harry stared at her a moment. He couldn't detect any guile or mockery in her eyes. Her question was sincere. Amelia Blackwell really did not recognize him. Not that that was a complete shock. The Blackwells and the Fletchers had never had much to do with each other above living in the same county.

A smile touched his lips. "I am proud to say that I hail from simple Godfrey Place near Ryhall. Not far from here, as a matter of fact. Are you a native to Rutland as well?"

Gussie ducked her head, her mouth tight. Had he made her smile again, or was she displeased?

Amelia had stilled, a confused look on her face. Harry watched as enlightenment finally struck her. "You are from *those* Fletchers? Oh! Forgive me. My stupid, foolish mind. How silly of me to have never made the connection. Oh, do forgive me, I beg."

Harry smiled and lifted a hand to say that all was forgiven. "It has been a long time since we've met. Think nothing of it."

"Yes, it must have been. Otherwise, I would have remembered. It must have been so long ago, for I feel sure I could never forget a face like yours."

Harry grinned at the attempted compliment and lost no time in lightening the conversation. "That ugly, eh?"

Next to him, Gussie shut her eyes and clenched her jaw. Sure signs she was trying not to laugh. But Amelia gasped. "No, not at all! I would never—as if I would—"

Harry laughed. "You're not the first person to point it out, I'll have you know." He quickly realized that Amelia was becoming seriously distressed and made haste to reassure her. "Forgive me, you don't know me well enough yet to laugh when I degrade myself for the amusement of others. It was only in fun."

Amelia looked as if she thought there was nothing funny about it but recovered a calm composure. "I see now. So funny. I don't know you well, it is true, but I hope that may be soon rectified. Are you fond of cards and dancing, sir?"

Gussie gathered up her reins and began backing up her horse to make a turn. "Mary is here. If you'll excuse me."

***

Any situation involving Amelia Blackwell was a situation that called for a hasty exit. So, the instant Gussie noticed her sister driving up in her phaeton, she made good of it and excused herself. Let Harry have all the time he'd like with Amelia.

Gussie had seen her father among the gentlemen and had given him no more than a salutary lift of her riding crop, which he had acknowledged with a lift of his head before returning his attention to his friends.

He and Gussie were fond of each other but in a distant way. Neither truly needed the other in their everyday lives. So long as Gussie didn't do anything to raise talk among the ton (an easy thing to do, when one locked oneself up in the library most days) and was seen in the saddle enough to suit him, Sir Gerald didn't have much to do with her life, which in turn suited her.

She had thought it rather cold of him to leave his wife so soon after she'd given him an heir. But if there was an epitome of a creature of habit, it was Sir Gerald. Fall and winter were for shooting and hunting, and so here he was, hunting and shooting, whether Phyllis and his daughters would join him or not.

But Mary—Mary was quite the opposite of their father. Always willing to please, even if it meant a great deal of discomfort to her. Gussie adored and pitied her at the same time, knowing better than anyone how Mary really felt under the strain she allowed herself to take on if it meant not displeasing others.

Gussie came up to the phaeton. She hadn't seen Mary since she'd come to Rutland. "Are you well, dearheart? And Diana and Phyllis?"

Mary's round cheeks lifted in a smile as she pressed her fingers against Gussie's outstretched hand that greeted her. "All well when we left." She leaned in and lowered her voice. "Diana and Hugh are falling more in love with each other every minute, it seems. You can see it is difficult for them to pretend they hardly know each other."

Gussie nodded in understanding. "They'll manage. Diana will make sure of that. And what of *your* recent endeavor? Have you had any luck with it?"

This question she whispered in a voice so low, so great a secret it was, that Mary had to lean down further to catch it. Her face fell a little. "I heard back from one just after you left. It was a no. A very decided no. I'm sure the others will be the same."

"But perhaps not."

Mary attempted to smile but it faded halfway. "I'm beginning to think it was a silly idea. I was a fool for even thinking I could do it."

"Hush. No such thing," Gussie said, admonishing Mary with her voice. "It's only one denial. Do not give up."

That was all the time they had to speak of Mary's secret endeavor. Gussie would never disclose it to anyone in the world. Not even Diana. It was Mary's secret, and only Mary would decide who knew it and who didn't.

There were too many people around them by now, and Squire Barrett was about to begin the hunt. Gussie and Mary moved over to where the women had gathered to see the men off.

She could tell Harry was getting most of the looks from the ladies. He was the mysterious heir to Camrose, come back from faraway lands, after all. Now that Harry was back and Mrs. Fletcher receiving visitors, their mourning for John complete, everyone in the neighborhood got to satisfy their curiosity about the new baronet. From the expressions on their faces and the little bits of conversation Gussie's ears picked up here and there, Harry was already making a favorable impression.

She studied him for a moment. With his strong frame, thick brown hair that curled slightly at the tips, and his cheerful face, Harry was a fine figure no matter where he was. However, to her critical gaze, Gussie could tell that he wasn't entirely comfortable in the saddle. He had never had much opportunity to ride before the army, much less after he joined. She hoped he wouldn't take a fall while they were out.

Several of the women were also casting looks at Rosy, who sat on her gelding in the middle of the pack of men, looking confident and calm in the saddle as she waited for her father to blow his horn and start the dogs off.

Gussie heard Amelia Blackwell murmur to a friend while nodding in Rosy's direction. "She will never marry, that's clear, if she keeps joining the men in all their sports. What will she do next, pray? Join them in the shooting? Such mannish behaviors," she said, ending on a *tsk*.

Gussie's mind turned this comment around a few times and soon came to a conclusion. "Actually," she said, addressing the two ladies. "It makes more sense that she would have a *better* chance at making a match with one of them simply due to the fact that she is spending more time with them than we are. We won't see them until well into the afternoon, whereas she will spend all day with them. As for mannish behavior, no such thing. She looks every bit a woman out there."

Amelia's eyes became steely. "Are you saying that she only hunts so she has a chance to set her cap to anyone she likes while there are no other ladies present?"

Gussie blinked. Anyone who knew Rosy knew she didn't give a fig for anything but the joy of galloping across the fields and soaring over walls and ditches. Leave it to a girl like Amelia to twist a perfectly logical explanation into something motivated by pure selfishness. A hot flash of defensiveness came over her for Rosy, but she knew better than to take the bait.

Instead, while she took a last look at how Harry was faring, she said, "Not at all. You must not have understood what I said. That is not surprising since you always had to have your lessons repeated to you at least twice. But I haven't the inclination to explain it to you. Look, they're off."

At that moment, Squire Barrett put his little horn to his lips and gave a mighty blow above the baying hounds, who took off running. There was a general cheer among the riders as they put their horses to a canter and followed the hounds. The ladies called out farewells to them, some, like Amelia, even waving a handkerchief.

Before anyone could interrupt them, Mary said, "Do put up your horse and come with me for a drive. We can have a nice little chat and catch up on all our family secrets for the rest of the morning."

Chapter Eight

In the drawing room, Gussie had chosen a seat next to the tall windows. Not only did they provide excellent light for her reading while the other ladies of the party chatted away, but she would also be able to see when the riders were on their way back.

Under the overcast sky, she now spotted them about a half-mile off before a rise in the land swallowed them from view. A few minutes later, they were nearly back on Lilford land.

Gussie closed her book and quietly stood and went to the door. Unassuming as her movements were, they stirred the attention of the other two girls seated by the windows to look out across the park. "The men are coming back," they cried.

Everyone went out to meet the returning party. Gussie's eyes quickly flitted over the riders until she found Rosy with a great smile plastered on her mud-spattered face. No worse for wear, there.

She looked for Harry next, which didn't take long for many of the other ladies had found him first and were asking him how he had fared. Since there was already a crowd around him, Gussie didn't move his way but looked on as they interacted.

Harry's coat had started out red but was now sporting big brown patches of mud caked all over him. He must have been in the back of the pack for much of the time. Looking harder, Gussie soon grew impatient with the other women. Why didn't they give him room to dismount? Why must they keep talking to him when it was clear he was exhausted? His movements were tender and disjointed. His shoulders were hitched up slightly and his torso stiff, as if he were bracing himself against the soreness he must be feeling after such a hard ride.

She felt an urge to walk up and scold the other ladies for being so unfeeling, but that probably wouldn't do any good and would call attention to her that she did not want. Fortunately, Rosy came up to her just then. "Come with me while I get changed. I need to talk to you."

The urgency in Rosy's voice intrigued Gussie, and she followed her friend up into the room designated for changing. Rosy's maid was already spreading a day dress out on the bed as they closed the door behind them.

"What happened?" Gussie asked. "No one was hurt, were they?"

"Sir Gerald's mount nearly toppled over Mr. Sydney when his horse refused a wall. The streaks his hooves made in the grass when he stopped might as well have been a mile long. I'll show them to you tomorrow."

"And how did Harry fare?"

Rosy pulled a face. "Harry is game as a pebble, we both know that, but anyone can see that he doesn't hunt or even ride much."

"He couldn't much, you know. It's not his fault."

"I know and I don't blame him for it. It only shows, that's all. Some of the men teased him relentlessly for his form when he jumped. We must positively do something about it," Rosy replied as she stripped off her gloves. The maid dipped a cloth in a bowl of hot water and wiped off the speckles of dried mud from Rosy's face with ruthless vigor.

"Why?"

"Gussie, you should have seen him. He stayed with us every step of the way. His pride wouldn't have allowed him to do anything else, but he cannot ride! I lost count how many times I thought he would come off his horse. I don't know how he sat through it when his horse balked at the ditch by Fengate Lane. But he became the laughingstock of the hunt. We have to help him. And I think I know how to do it."

Gussie took a chair. She did not like the idea of all the other men laughing at Harry. He probably had been laughing at himself right along with them, but the very thought of it made her jaw go tight. "How?"

Rosy stood still while her maid began extracting her out of her habit. "We're going to ride with him every morning, if he's agreeable. No, even if he's not, we'll force him out with us. You and I can school him on his seat, and we know where all the best jumps are. We simply must help him. He won't last another hunt if we do not."

Gussie thought for a moment. "Are you saying this to indeed help him, or were you just embarrassed for him?"

"Both! But what do you think? You'll meet him at the south field between Broadstone and Camrose with me in the morning, won't you?"

"Of course I will. If you can get him there."

"Oh, but won't you ask him? He always listened to you, and I have a feeling that he still thinks I'm still only fifteen."

Gussie furrowed her brow in amused confusion. "What makes you say that?"

"Just the way he speaks to me. I don't think he realizes that I've grown up."

"You're still the madcap you were when you were fifteen."

Rosy pulled a face at her before she disappeared into the day dress her maid threw over her head. She reappeared a moment later. "Yes, but now I am a more grown up one. It doesn't bother me, really. I only noticed it. It's rather funny. But if we are to help him, you'd better ask him. Will you? It will be like old times, just the three of us."

Thinking back to the group of ladies surrounding him upon the hunt's return, Gussie had a feeling that Harry's time would not be his own. There was going to be some competition for his attention that had not been there when they were children. "I'll talk to him. But if he doesn't wish for it, I'm not going to compel him. You'll have to take over from there."

"Done," Rosy said with a nod. She turned to her maid. "Are *you* quite done with me?"

"No, miss, there's still your hair to do. I'll have a time combing out the mud you have in the back, so I tell you now."

Rosy slouched her shoulders in impatience but remained still. "Gussie, will you go find Harry, then? We need to help him, really."

Gussie rose from her chair. "Very well, I shall see what he thinks of this plan of yours. Though be prepared; he may not fancy a girl teaching him, now that he is a man. It's different now."

"If it were different, then he would treat me like I am a grown woman and not the child he left behind. Does he talk to you like you're still sixteen?"

"No," Gussie answered, but she had been talking to him for years through their letters. She couldn't remind Rosy of that in front of her maid though, and so she went downstairs on that answer to seek Harry out.

***

After changing, Harry had taken refuge on an upholstered bench behind a giant potted palm plant that hugged the stairs in Lilford's entry hall. As he sat down, his whole body protested at the movement yet relaxed wonderfully once he got off his feet. He was eager to join the rest of the party once he had changed but did need a few minutes respite.

The hunt had taken more out of him than he'd expected, and he was already beginning to feel its effects. He had thought riding for a few hours couldn't be that much different than marching and running drills all day, but his body was fast telling him it was otherwise. By morning, his inner thighs would make walking an absolute misery, he was sure. When was the next hunt?

He tilted his head back until it touched the staircase and closed his eyes. They were beginning to droop anyway. He could hear the swish of someone's skirts at the top of the stairs and the soft patter of slippers touching the carpet as the lady descended. He prayed that he would go unnoticed until he was ready.

A few beats of silence told him that the moment of detection had passed. He took in a deep breath and let it slowly seep out of him. Just one minute more and he would get up...

"What are you hiding back there for?"

Harry's eyes shot open. Gussie's cool, collected figure was right in front of him. "How did you do that?"

She cocked her head. "Do what?"

"Was that you coming down the stairs? I heard that. Why didn't I hear you coming up to me?"

"Likely because you were asleep," she replied.

Harry frowned. "I was not."

"You were. It was a wonder your mouth wasn't dropped open, it was so slack. But never mind that."

Harry was about to mind that, but Gussie stepped up to the bench and sat down next to him. He quickly shifted to make room on the small seat. There wasn't much. The skirt of her dress brushed against his pantaloons, though they were not touching. That feeling of *home* settled onto him as he watched her arrange her seat to her liking. It felt good to have her so near. "What is it?" he asked.

"How was your ride?"

"Not bad."

"Did you enjoy it?"

"Yes," he said after a moment's hesitation. He would be cursing it in the morning.

She narrowed her eyes at him. She had noticed. "And are you looking forward to the next hunt at Whitehead?"

Harry's eyes narrowed in return at her sweet tone. "Yes."

"It's only in three days' time."

"Gussie, why all the questions? Get to what you really want to tell me."

She jerked her head in a firm nod. "Right. Rosy says you looked abominable out there in the saddle, and we have a mind to ride with you each morning so we can school you."

Harry lowered his head and looked a question under his brow. "You're going to school me?"

"Well, I'm not. Rosy will. She told me they were laughing at you half the time out there. You cannot have liked it. I should hate it if they were laughing at me. I couldn't bear it."

Harry took the precaution of not laughing at her now, though a small smile spread across his mouth. One of her greatest fears, being laughed at. Though he could rather have done without all the mocking, Harry wouldn't have cried off from the hunt for the world. Hunting was a new challenge that he was looking forward to mastering, even if he wasn't enjoying it now.

But to have two women offering to make him a better rider pricked his pride a little. There was no reason why he should be better than them. Gussie and Rosy had been put in the saddle by their fathers before they could even walk. He pushed his smarting feelings aside for a moment. "What are the two of you offering, exactly?"

"Just to ride with you each morning."

"Starting when?"

"Tomorrow, if that suits."

Harry could almost hear his body scream that it would *not* suit. But the thought of riding out, just the three of them—that was something he did want. The feelings he had surrounding Gussie were recent, and he couldn't tell if they were here because he had been gone for so long, or if they were something else altogether. Something stronger.

He wanted to find out.

He glanced down at the scar on his hand. Perhaps a chance to clear the air around the Pact would arise out of it, for the more he thought about it, the surer he was that Gussie remembered it. She remembered nearly everything.

He lifted his hand and offered it to Gussie. "That suits fine."

Gussie looked him a question before putting her hand in his. "Really? That's it, then?"

Harry closed his hand around hers, giving it a firm shake. His mind registered just how soft and smooth her skin felt against his. An urge to bring up the Pact here and now came over him. No one had come across them yet. They were still alone, but that could change at any minute out in the open of the hall. He knew a discussion about the Pact would take more time than they had.

Besides, while they had only been sitting together for a few minutes, they were half-hidden by a potted plant. That could be seen as clandestine. Anyone happening upon them might come to the wrong conclusions. "That's it, then. Where are you going now? I'm expected in the billiard room until luncheon. Do you want to watch?"

***

May 1812

> *...I tried my hand at the pungi a while back. Have you heard of that instrument? The men here use it to charm cobras out of baskets. I wouldn't have believed it if I had not seen it myself. With my playing, I think the cobra would either kill me straight off or retreat in the other direction. Anything to get away from the sound I was making...*

When Mrs. Barrett was informed that Rosy and Gussie were engaged to ride out with Harry nearly every morning, she beamed. "That is good of you, indeed, Rose. Sir Harry has been gone for so long, I feel sure he would be grateful to have a guide to help reacquaint himself with the country."

Rosy wrinkled her nose. "I don't think Harry's been gone so long as to have forgotten the place where he grew up. Nothing's changed, has it, Gussie?"

"Not much," Gussie said before Mrs. Barrett could reply.

Pursing her lips a trifle, Mrs. Barrett didn't let that dissuade her. "That is just the sort of attentiveness I was talking about before, you know."

It was discovered that Rosy was not the only one who had thought to help Harry acclimate back into English country life.

The next morning, he was already waiting for them at the designated lane that separated Broadstone land from Camrose. After hailing them with a jolly good morning, Harry said, "I can only ride for an hour."

Rosy scoffed. "An hour? That's hardly enough time to do anything."

"Says you," Harry retorted.

"You must have business, then?" Gussie asked. "We can forgive him for that, surely, Rosy?" Though if she were being honest, she found she would have preferred more time with him as well. Indeed, she had found herself smiling at the prospect as she readied herself that morning. But of course, Harry had a great deal of business just now. She could perfectly understand that his time was not his own.

"Actually, I'm engaged to drive out with Mr. Sydney and his lot. I'm taking Miss Blackwell in the curricle."

Gussie's expression froze. "You're taking Amelia Blackwell out?"

"Yes. And after that, it is tea at Whitehead Hall with the baron and his family. Amy and Charlotte are acquainted with his daughters, did you know that?"

"You're certainly busy," Rosy said.

Harry nodded. "Everyone has been very welcoming."

Gussie found that she did not much like people and their neighborly kindnesses, but what could she say? Harry did not belong to her. "We'd better get on with our ride since we only have you for so long. Rosy, start your teaching."

Harry gave Rosy an exaggerated bow. "I am at your service."

Rosy, with a wicked grin, soon had him posting down the lane with them at a smart trot. Gussie studied his form as he rose up and down in the saddle in rhythm with the horse's strides. Through the fashionable, tight buckskins of the day, she could see his muscles bulge and strain as he tried to sync his own movements with those of his gelding.

Harry's eye caught her own and then looked down at his thighs. The grin that followed along with his wagging brows made her shoot her gaze straight ahead of her. It wouldn't do to stare and study for so long, even if it was Harry. *Especially* if it was Harry. He was one of her best friends, after all.

Heat crept into her cheeks as she heard him let out a chuckle. She must say something, or he would run away with the wrong idea. "I was studying your form, Harry, nothing more. You flatter yourself if you think otherwise."

"Of course, Gussie. I absolutely believe that my shapely leg was not the object of your scrutiny just now," he replied with an overabundance of sincerity.

Gussie sighed. He had not only run away with the wrong idea, he was halfway round the world with it. She gave a grand roll of her eyes but kept her gaze straight ahead. Harry's laughter confirmed that he had seen it.

Even with his imperfect form, Gussie admitted to herself that he cut a very fine figure astride a horse. She hoped that he would mark the flush in her cheeks down to the cold morning. She had already conceded that Harry was handsome. It was old information now, so why was she having to stifle a flock of butterflies in her stomach?

"Harry! Mind your seat," Rosy barked.

Harry looked their way with a grimace. "Are we done yet?"

Rosy now rolled her eyes at him but laughed. They weren't even ten minutes in.

There now, Gussie thought. *Harry isn't so much handsome as he is amusing, and that makes him attractive to anyone.*

That had to be it. Harry was funny. She just needed to remind herself, though she found the thought a hard one to hold onto.

Rosy called out corrections here and there, but anyone could see that with enough time Harry would be just as good a rider as the next gentleman. This realization made room for more conversation and banter between the three friends. Rosy and Harry opened their mouths at Gussie's reporting of the accident in London only a few weeks ago that people were now calling The Beer Flood. Rosy gave them a report on the broodmares in her father's stables and fields and which ones she thought would produce the best foals come spring. And Harry gave a detailed description of differences in riding an elephant as opposed to a horse.

Toward the end of their ride, as they circled back to Broadstone, they passed the big birch tree by the pond in one of the paddocks. Gussie stared at the place as they rode by. It was under that tree that she and Harry had made their pact all those years ago. She and Harry had played under and passed the tree plenty of times since then, but this time was different. The Pact had actually been fulfilled. She dashed a quick look at him. Would he recognize the spot? Had he even seen it? And what if he did? Would anything happen? *Please bring it up,* Gussie pleaded in her head. *Please bring it up so I don't have to...*

A week passed with them all enjoying a morning ride together each day, marking Harry's progress. Some days they were alone, other days they would ride with others whom they happened upon in the neighborhood. The next hunt came and went with no accident (though Harry was still the butt of plenty of jokes).

Gussie's enjoyment was only marred by one thing: every time Harry escorted them back to Broadstone, they would pass the place where the Pact had been made. Each time Harry went by it unnoticing, a weight settled on her shoulders, growing heavier and heavier each day.

She should just say something and get it over with. Perhaps she would look foolish to him by bringing it up, especially if he didn't remember, but she should release him from any obligation he might feel. A promise was a promise, after all, and it fell to her to acquit Harry of any obligation he may feel from having made such a preposterous vow.

Was that really what she wanted to do? The thought of marriage had always been distasteful to her, but she thought she could manage it if it weren't for the children that would most assuredly follow. It wasn't the actual children she was afraid of, after all, but the process of bringing them into the world.

She could feel her chest tighten and her heart pick up speed as she remembered how Phyllis had looked even a day after her travail when Gussie had visited her to see her new half-brother. The state she had been in, languishing against the pillows, completely exhausted and nearly helpless to do anything by herself, simply horrified Gussie, whose memory of the foaling had made her pace up and down her room during Phyllis's confinement, wondering if the process would kill her.

Phyllis's temper had increased tenfold as well, snapping at the servants, Sir Gerald (who had quickly taken the hint and stayed away from his wife as much as he could), and even Gussie and her sisters, though Gussie could tell she tried to hold her tongue a little during their visits to her room.

If that was what babies did to a woman, Gussie wanted no part in it. She was not used to pain, and a noisy, bothersome infant did not seem worth the misery it took to bring them into the world. So, if she didn't want children, it followed that she could not want marriage.

Perhaps she could marry Harry and be happy with him. He would doubtless try to make her laugh several times a day, but if they were married, she would not mind it so. Or it might drive her mad. But he would want children. *Needed* children to pass his new title to, and so would not be happy with her if she refused him that.

She had her answer, she supposed. But she was getting ahead of herself. They hadn't even so much as mentioned the Pact yet. Perhaps he would tell her outright that he thought nothing of it now and would not marry her for the world. Who knew? But then, it's not as if he would be getting married tomorrow. He had only just returned to England. Likely it would be a few years before he began to think of a wife, especially since he was still so young.

But when he did marry, would she lose the friendship they had? Would that change? If he married someone else, they could no longer ride together and talk together with such freedom as they did now, could they? Did she really want that? Could she give him up? Another question struck her mind like a clap of thunder.

After he married, would he burn her letters?

Would she have to burn his?

"Do you remember that place?"

Harry's words startled her out of her thoughts. She looked at him, then to where he was pointing. The birch tree.

Good lord, he was bringing it up.

They were by themselves. Silvertail had been excessively unruly during their hack, and Rosy was working him up and down the lane while Gussie and Harry waited for her, alone for all intents and purposes. And now here he was finally mentioning the place whose only importance had been the Pact. She would finally be relieved of the weight that had been pressing on her mind since Harry had come back. After that, they could go on as they had always done before, and everything would be well.

Until he married...

She panicked.

"That place? Where?" she asked. Her voice came out like a squeak.

Harry emphasized his pointing finger with a jerk of his arm. "There. The tree. Do you remember what happened there, Gussie?"

His softened tone sent Gussie's heart pounding against her ribs. Her entire frame vibrated from the tremors it produced. Her eyes widened as she tried to swallow. Her throat had gone dry. "Why I—erm—isn't that—"

The softer light that touched his eyes, and the smile that started to grow on Harry's face at her stammering only amplified her alarm.

"You broke your arm falling from that tree, remember?" she said in a rush, desperate to get something out.

Harry's face quirked up. "No, was it? I thought that happened at Godfrey Place..."

It most certainly had happened at Harry's very own house, but Gussie's panic had taken the bit between its teeth and was bolting away with her common sense. "No, I am sure it was that tree. You must have climbed every tree within five miles of us, but that was the one you fell out of."

Her heart hammered in her ears, making it hard to hear. She desperately hoped Harry wouldn't notice her shallow breathing or her fidgeting eyes. She looked over his shoulder to see how close Rosy was. Silvertail looked to be minding her now, and she was making her way back to them. Coming, but not close enough.

She felt Harry's eyes on her, and resolutely met them with her own. His brows were set low, and his jaw jutted out in a contemplative manner. He set a hand on his hip and turned back to look at the birch. He looked back at her. "Really?"

Gussie swallowed and nodded. "Yes, that was what happened there. Do you remember your mother shooing me away when I asked if I could watch the doctor set the bone? She called me an unnatural girl and sent me home."

That drew a laugh from Harry. "Yes, and it was an apt description of you." He looked to the tree with hard, searching eyes once more. "Though I could have sworn..."

He said nothing more, for Rosy had finally reached them. A pit formed in Gussie's stomach. Harry would almost definitely ask Rosy if that was indeed the tree he fell from. Then Gussie, cursing herself, would have to continue the lie to them both, and she was sorely lacking in slyness. She always told the truth, and when she could not, she chose not to say anything at all rather than lie. What a fix she had just gotten herself into. What was wrong with her?

"Thank you for waiting," Rosy said as she pulled Silvertail up. "I don't know why he acted up so, but he is better now."

"He caught a scent of something he didn't like?" Gussie asked. A change of subject was imperative.

"Perhaps, but the other horses didn't act up."

"Perhaps he saw a ghost?" Harry suggested.

"Very funny. Ghosts only come out at night. Besides, our part of the county is not haunted, more's the pity. He must not be feeling quite the thing. I hope you weren't bored to death while you waited for me."

"Not at all," Harry replied. "We were just—"

Alarm seized Gussie's lungs. Quickly she said, "Not bored, but we must get back home, Rosy. I need to write to Diana before we go into the village with your mother. I promised I would write faithfully, and I've been horribly remiss." She turned Brutus toward Broadstone and put her heel to him. "Until next time, Harry."

Behind her, Rosy made a noise of surprise before Silvertail's hoof-beats told Gussie she was following her. "Goodbye, Harry," Rosy called. "We shall see you at Welbeck's ball, shall we not?"

"Looking forward to it." Harry's deep voice vibrated in Gussie's head.

She gritted her teeth. That could have gone much, *much* smoother.

Chapter Nine

I have taken up the harp under severe duress. Diana and the governess cornered me in the upstairs sitting room and told me I had to pick some other instrument besides the pianoforte, and it was to be the harp. I should think that one instrument should suffice for someone who is going to live alone for the rest of her life, shouldn't you?

After they rejected my suggestions of the sitar and pungi, or even the guitar, we negotiated with the result that I would take up the harp and cast off any and all needlework and use those hours in the library instead. They neither of them have even heard of a pungi, but I think I should like it better than the harp. I'd take most anything over the harp.

A perplexed frown accompanied Harry all the way back to Camrose. Gussie's certainty had had him questioning himself while he was with her, but the more he thought about it, the more certain he was.

He had broken his arm falling from the tree in his own garden at Godfrey Place. How else would his mother have sent Gussie away? If it had happened at Broadstone, that meant he would have had to walk all the way home with a broken arm, and he hadn't done that. His mother had been at his side almost an instant later. John had come out and laughed at him. His little sisters had cried.

Why was Gussie so sure it had been *that* tree?

He had been ready to broach the Pact with her. It had felt like the right moment, being so close to where it had taken place. In bringing it up, he thought he could make a case not to hold her to her promise, but to ask her to give him a chance.

But Gussie had not reacted at all how he'd thought she would. He had expected a little embarrassment, but then the usual forthright manner with which she took most every other subject. He had never known her to balk at any question put to her. Did it mean that she wanted to keep the Pact, or not? It was a puzzlement that followed him all the way home.

When he came to the Camrose stables, he put on a brave face in front of the groom while he dismounted. He would never admit it out loud, but Harry was unsure whether he would be able to walk without considerable pain for the rest of his life.

Riding every day with Gussie and Rosy had been beneficial in many ways, but the last hunt had still been hard on him. Like on his first hunt, he had kept up with the other riders but was still paying for it two days later. And tonight, dancing was on the docket. The Welbeck's were hosting a private supper and ball. He wondered how much his stiff legs would allow him to do.

But Gussie would be there, and they were engaged to dance the first two dances.

That night, Sloane, his bateman he had brought with him from India, had everything at the ready needed to dress Harry for an evening of finery and refinement. "We'll turn you into a proper valet if you're not careful," he jested.

Sloane's face soured, the lines of over twenty years in the Indian sun having deepened his already expressive face. He picked up the horsehair brush from the tray and swiped at Harry's coat, removing any stray hairs. "If a man can't get 'is coat on by 'isself, 'e's not a man, I say."

Harry laughed. "I promise I won't turn the dandy on you. I couldn't play the part if I tried. But there's many a lady who prefer them, I'm told."

Sloane shrugged. "Plenty of women who don't want a man dressing as pretty as them. You keep to that Scott fellow I've heard about instead of Weston and you'll get on. Someone's bound to take a fancy to you. But I'll say it's a good thing you're rich."

Harry threw a good-natured scowl in the bateman's direction before reaching for the only adornment he had: his father's watch. Since settling in at Camrose, several women had come to be introduced to Sir Harry who wouldn't have given plain Harry Fletcher, or even Corporal Fletcher a second glance. Doubtless that would please his mother, but Harry didn't like it.

How was he to tell if it was really him whom they wanted to know or his title?

He dismissed Sloane a few moments later but stayed up in his room for a little solitude. There was still time before the carriage would be ready to bear him and his family to the Welbeck's for the evening.

Though he wanted nothing more than to sit and rest, he kept himself up and walking about the room, giving his muscles less of a chance to stiffen up. As he did so, he remembered something and slipped his hand inside his coat to an inner pocket. He had been reading one of Gussie's letters when he'd last worn this coat and had forgotten to put it back with the others. The edges of the paper were thin and dog-eared with little tears here and there— partly from travel, but mostly from his reading it so much. Most of his letters from her had the same look.

Once his grief had lessened its grip on him, one of the first things he'd taken up after John's death was a letter from Gussie. An older one, written while John was still alive.

While his military duties didn't change much after John was buried, they didn't offer much in the way of taking his brother off his mind. John and the army went hand in hand and always would. But Gussie's matter-of-fact accounts of life back in England worked as a balm to his sorrow. Her questions about India helped take his mind off his grief, and her thoughts about the books she was reading at the time or no-nonsense opinions about whatever scandal might be rocking the boat among the ton during her time in London made him laugh. The letter in his hand set a smile off as she complained about her harp lessons.

Through their letters, Gussie had become a better friend to him than he could have looked for. When he'd received the belated news of his cousin George's death only a few weeks after John's, one of his first thoughts after realizing that *he* had inherited Camrose was an almost overwhelming desire not to fulfill the Pact, but to just get back to Gussie.

Harry returned the letter to its place. Would she have him, though?

If Harry had had his way, he and his mother and sisters would have arrived at the ball in a timely manner. But all his orderly years in the army could not contend with three women preparing for a ball.

Arriving at Mr. Welbeck's home and greeting their hosts, Amy and Charlotte lost no time in finding their friends among the younger set of people there who were to be entertained mostly upstairs. Harry and Mrs. Fletcher lingered with Mr. and Mrs. Welbeck a little longer exchanging pleasantries and complimenting them on the rooms decked out for the occasion. "I've never seen so many flowers in November," Mrs. Fletcher said.

Mrs. Welbeck beamed with pride. "They are most of them from my own hot houses in the garden. I cannot abide the dullness of winter in the country without my flowers."

Mr. Welbeck and Harry had been exchanging pleasantries when Squire Barrett came up to them. Slapping a hand on his old friend's shoulder, he said to Mr. Welbeck, "Cards are at the ready whenever you are. Sir Harry, you'll join us, won't you?"

Harry gave a nod in apology. "I am dancing first. Perhaps I'll steal in there later."

At that moment, Mrs. Welbeck turned to the men and addressed herself to Mr. Barrett. "Squire, I have just remembered. I would ask her myself, but I haven't seen your daughter since she came. Can you persuade her to play for us tonight?"

The squire shook his head. "I am afraid she's never learnt any instrument well enough to play for anyone but the barn cats. Though she might sing. If we open the windows, the dogs in the yard might even join in."

They all laughed at the squire's description of his daughter's talents. Harry had a feeling that had she heard her father, with his gentle teasing tone, Rosy would have laughed the most of all.

"I had forgotten she is not fond of music much," said Mrs. Welbeck. "But, Mr. Welbeck, it is terribly vexing. All the girls seem to favor the pianoforte tonight even with that lovely harp sitting in the corner. Only our daughter has consented to play it."

"Oh, Gussie—Miss Stilwell, you know, *she* plays the harp," Harry said, eager to help.

***

Gussie and the Barrett family had been late getting to the Welbeck's. A lost glove had sent the whole household on a frenzied search ("Really, Rosy, how could you manage to lose just one glove? They are a pair. They are always meant to stay together!" Mrs. Barrett had cried).

Once she had stepped past her hosts and into the rooms, all opened and decked with arrangements of flowers whose fragrance she was sure would make her nauseous before the night's end, Gussie looked for Harry. She had to find him first. She didn't want to be surprised by him popping up beside her.

What had she been thinking that day? She had been waiting and waiting, hoping that he would bring up the Pact between them, and when he finally had, *she* had completely panicked! The incident had taken up all the space in her head reserved for reading, writing, or anything productive.

She didn't want things to change, to lose the friendship they'd cultivated over a lifetime. A sentiment like that was all well and good, but in the back of her mind, she knew that things had already changed and would continue to do so. The discomfort of this was getting hard to manage.

Harry would marry. He might choose someone she didn't like and who didn't like her, like Amelia Blackwell. But if they went through with the Pact and married each other, that would change things as well, and the ever-present thought of children sent a shiver through her.

"Gussie! there you are."

She jumped and whirled around. Drat her wretched mind! Always flying her away to hypotheticals and making it impossible to attend to her surroundings. Harry had snuck up on her after all. He must have just arrived.

"Hello, Harry," she said, dipping a small curtsy.

Harry grabbed her hand and strode past her. "I need to tell you something, follow me."

Wide-eyed at the urgency in his voice, Gussie followed, but was half inclined to tear her arm away from his grasp and run the other way. What was he going to tell her? He couldn't possibly think that this was the time to bring up the Pact in the middle of a ball. What if he made a scene? What if he knelt at her feet and told her he loved her in front of...

Loved her?

That thought had never entered her head before.

Before she could become wholly terrified of this new thought and what it might mean, Harry stopped. He had taken her to the far corner of the drawing room next to, as it turned out, a fake potted orange tree. As he turned to face her, she braced herself. What was he going to say?

"I'm sorry for it, but I told Mrs. Welbeck you play the harp, and she's going to ask you to play for everyone tonight."

Gussie's mouth opened in dismay but the air in her lungs seemed to rush out by way of her feet. "Harry, you didn't! Oh no! *That* was why she looked at me so when we greeted her. Harry!"

"I said I'm sorry. It just came out. I was reading—" He stopped short. Gussie would have gone on berating him, but he continued, lowering his voice. "I remembered you mentioning it in your letters but didn't remember that you hated the thing until after I'd told Mrs. Welbeck."

"She didn't ask how you knew, did she? I only took it up two years ago and *you*, I will remind you, have been gone for four. How would you know I took up the harp if we *have not been in contact with one another?*" She muttered her question through gritted teeth. If anything could make her stop thinking about what might happen if Harry fell in love with her, it was that wretched instrument.

"I know, but I wanted to help."

"You did not help!"

"I helped her," he said with an apologetic shrug.

Gussie shut her eyes as anger closed in on her good will. She brought up her hands and grasped his arms. "I could shake you for being so careless."

Indeed, she tried. Harry moved but little. When had he become so solid?

Harry looked from one of her hands to the other. "Want to try again?" he asked, amusement brimming over in his eyes.

She snatched her hands back to her sides, remembering they were in a room full of people. He took a step closer to her. Now she had to tilt her chin up even more to meet his eye. She did so, and the way he looked down at her made her still.

"I am sorry, Gussie," he said, a smile, mostly hidden by his mustache, lurking up one side of his face. "It came out without thinking. But I, for one, would like to hear you play."

With that soft request, she could feel her frustration toward him begin to seep away. She sighed and pinched a fold of her dress between her fingers. "There's no harm in it, I suppose. I may hate the harp but that doesn't mean everyone else does as well."

"Quite right." Harry grinned, but that certain look in his eye Gussie had noticed after she shook him (or tried to, anyway) actually deepened as he shifted his feet. "Gussie, if we could, I'd like to—"

He paused, looking down to the floor. She waited with a growing unease in her stomach. What did he want to say? What could he say with so many people surrounding them? Why was he making her feel this way?

"Yes," she prompted, not entirely sure she wanted to.

Harry raised his eyes back to her face and huffed out a laugh. "It's nothing, only...didn't we do the silliest things as children?" He lifted his left hand up and with his other hand rubbed the scar he had made with that dull knife of his all those years ago. "We did some of the most outrageous things, don't you think?"

Like making a blood pact?

Even after all these years, Gussie had never understood why she had agreed to such a gruesome ritual. She looked from his hand to him and back again. "Yes, horribly ill-advised. One might even say stupid?" She narrowed her eyes. Was that what he was getting at?

"Incredibly stupid," he said, his eyes twinkling. "Anyone with any sense wouldn't give another thought to such things, nor hold anyone involved to their word, would they?"

This was it. She understood now. He was releasing her from any obligation the Pact might have had on her. She felt the relief inside her burst from the cage it had been trapped in since Harry had come back. She gave him something that she hoped resembled a grateful smile. "One would be a nincompoop if one did."

Harry chuckled. "Yes, that's just how I feel about it." He raised his eyes and looked about the room. Gussie looked too and saw that other guests were coming toward them.

Harry looked back at her. "I'll make sure my sister is in the room while you're playing. She is one of those who loves the harp, you know. And remember, you still have to dance with me. You promised."

He wagged a finger at her for emphasis. Normally an action like that might make her lips twitch, but she was in no mood for games just now. "Get you away, Harry Fletcher," she said a little breathlessly. "And I did not practice my steps like you asked me to. My apologies."

She held back the desire to give him a shove, as she had done plenty of times as a child. There were too many eyes that could see them, and an innocent touch seen by the wrong person could bring about talk and gossip that was exhausting just to think about, much less navigate through.

Harry smiled, though. She had never known him to rein a smile in. "Put some padding in your slippers, for half the time I still feel I'm on that blasted boat being rocked about to and fro. My apologies in advance."

That one hit home. Gussie's chest caved in and a huff of laughter escaped her right as Amelia Blackwell and her mother came up to them. The satisfaction on Harry's face as he turned his attention to the other ladies was palpable. Leave it to Harry to never stop until his target lost control and made a fool of oneself.

Chapter Ten

June 1813

> *Do you know what happens when a gun misfires near an un-suspecting elephant? Well, let this be a lesson to always keep your rifle cleaned. That fellow is an absolute...if you were really Gus Stillman, I would say what he was, but to you, Gussie, he is an absolute nincompoop!*

Gussie did not have another opportunity to speak to Harry before the gong sounded for dinner. The other women of the party would not let him out of the circle they'd formed about him. They asked him all sorts of questions, begging to be told about India. The tales he regaled them with were ones Gussie already knew, so she stayed by Rosy's side and made a study of the group instead.

The flock of women seemed entranced. Even her sister Mary was listening with fixed eyes to Harry's account of an elephant stampeding through the camp one afternoon. She remembered that story from his letters—and how much work his regiment had to do in the aftermath.

She had known a feeling of displeasure at seeing him surrounded by so many ladies both young and old, but in another way, this was a good thing. The more he spoke of India, the more others would know of his adventures. Gussie wouldn't have to watch her tongue quite as much when it came to Harry. If she slipped and said something Harry had written to only her, she could just say he had told her himself, which was perfectly true.

Rosy leaned over to Gussie's ear and murmured, "Amelia Blackwell, she's standing rather a bit *too* close to him, don't you think?"

Indeed, Amelia Blackwell's arm, encased in a long, white evening glove, was nearly touching Harry's. At that moment Harry must have said something funny because all the women laughed as much as their strict upbringings would allow. Amelia went so far as to lay her fan on his shoulder.

Gussie's eyes narrowed.

Beside her, Rosy had much the same expression on her face. She looked at Gussie. "Oh, I want to go over there and shove her. What makes her think she can do that with our Harry?"

On the inside, Gussie couldn't have agreed more with her friend. But the more steadied part of her mind soon schooled her irrational thoughts. It made perfect sense. "Very likely she and her mother have the same wishes toward Harry as your mother does. But you are not jealous, are you?" That was a new thought. Maybe Rosy *did* like Harry more than she let on but wouldn't admit it. "Harry won't choose a bride tomorrow. It will be years before he is ready to marry."

"Jealous? No, not at all. I don't love him, I told you. It is not jealousy. It is more...protective, I think. He's *our* friend, not Amelia's. And if she thinks to marry him, well, I'd have something to say about that."

"If you had a say in it at all, which you don't. Neither of us do."

"Harry would listen to you. He always did. Why *don't* you marry him? That would keep us all together as friends and nothing would change. We would all stay close to each other and ride out every morning. And you wouldn't have to teach your children to ride. I could do that for you."

Gussie shooed away the images Rosy was putting into her head. "Stop being ridiculous, do. You won't be at Broadstone forever. What if you should marry?"

"I only fall in love with handsome grooms, remember?" Rosy laughed. "Not that there are any handsome grooms in the stables at present. No, I shan't ever marry, I suppose. Just like you. Only you really should marry Harry. He's always liked you."

Rosy's flippancy was beginning to get on Gussie's nerves. It was time to turn the tables. "And what if your brother's friend were to suddenly show up again, hm? What was his name? Harrington, I believe?"

Rosy's mirthful expression dulled instantly. "That's not fair."

Gussie shrugged. "Just reminding you that you don't *only* fall in love with grooms."

The gong for dinner sounded, and the company split themselves into pairs based on position and rank to go into dinner. Harry was toward the front, taking one of the distinguished matrons into the dining room. Gussie was taken in with a friend of her father's whom she had known from her cradle.

Dinners could be a severe trial to Gussie, who, thanks to the free rein she'd had in the library after escaping her governess, had informed opinions about almost every topic under the sun. But she had made a promise to Diana not to ruffle so many feathers in social settings. It gave people a shock to hear a woman speak so fluently on Greek texts or what she thought of a commentary on Julius Caesar. It was not long into her first season that Gussie had been marked down as a bluestocking, and a disagreeable one at that.

She didn't show much reserve in talking about what she had learnt and would correct anyone, man or woman, if she thought they were wrong. Not one offer of marriage had been extended to her in the two years since she had been out, no matter how hard her female relatives tried. Several serious conversations with Diana and their aunt, who'd witnessed her societal faux pa,s had finally extracted a promise from Gussie that she would keep her opinions to herself, especially at someone else's dining room table.

As much as Gussie chafed against it, she felt the effects of keeping her tongue almost immediately. People would talk to her if she kept to the fashionable subjects of the day, as she was doing at the Welbeck's table now. She found it easiest to catch onto a topic that the guests to her right and left found interesting and simply let them talk about it.

Gussie passed the meal in this manner until Mrs. Welbeck led the ladies into the drawing room, where she lost no time in taking Gussie aside. "I have been informed that you play the harp, Miss Stilwell. Would you favor us with a demonstration tonight? Do say you will."

Mrs. Welbeck was as well-mannered and likable a lady as one could hope for in a neighbor. Combined with Harry's particular desire to hear her play, this kind request melted Gussie's resistance to the instrument enough for her to agree.

"Splendid. Thank you, my dear." Mrs. Welbeck said. "Your skills on the pianoforte give me high hopes that we will enjoy this just as much."

Gussie smiled graciously in return, but her expression turned to one of worry as she made her way to Rosy.

"But you hate the harp," Rosy said after Gussie told her what Harry had done.

"It cannot be helped. But I have not played in so long. I would rather not have my fumbling fingers make a fool of me in front of everyone."

When the gentlemen came in smelling of cigars and port, Mrs. Welbeck lost no time beginning the entertainments. To Gussie's dismay, her hostess ordered the harp to be brought out front and center. "Miss Augusta Stilwell, if you would be so kind as to play us a little something first?"

***

Ooh, she didn't like that.

Anyone watching Gussie as closely as Harry was would have noticed the stiffening of her neck and shoulders as Mrs. Welbeck called her up to the harp. But she placed herself on the stool with, if not confidence, certainly with grace, and brought the instrument to lean against her shoulder.

After a few practice plucks of the strings, she began playing. The room was enveloped with the liquid chords Gussie sent floating up into the air. She may hate the harp, but Harry couldn't help thinking how beautiful she looked as her arms moved so smoothly back and forth while her fingers found the proper strings.

He made himself take his eyes off her to glance about the room, curious to see how others were reacting. There were pleasant expressions on most of the guests' faces. Sir Gerald and Mr. Welbeck had their heads together, probably talking about horses or racing curricles or some such thing. His mother looked pleased by the music. Would this perhaps soften her heart toward Gussie a little?

Harry looked to his sister Amy next and found her completely entranced. He needed to get her and Charlotte up to London to learn from the masters there. Or engage a governess, at the very least, who could teach them all the accomplishments that they hadn't yet had the chance to learn.

There were a few faces that didn't look as pleased with Gussie's playing as the others. Not many, but one or two of the young ladies had a pinched look about their mouths. Miss Blackwell, who had sat beside him at dinner, sat straight as a rod looking at the far wall with a single brow lifted as if she were annoyed by how boring she thought the whole thing was.

Gussie played her last notes with an artistic flourish of her hands and slowly lowered them back to her sides as the music faded away. Applause immediately followed. Harry tried not to let his enthusiasm show by clapping the loudest and fastest, but it was a difficult thing. Gussie accepted the praise with a few nods of her head to the guests before standing the harp up straight and rising from the stool. A footman came to move the harp back to its corner while she returned to Rosy.

Mrs. Welbeck rose. "Miss Stilwell, thank you. What a treat, indeed." She called the next performer to the pianoforte. There was a general shifting of the room as guests refilled their teacups or moved over to speak to another acquaintance. Harry saw Amy make her way over to Gussie, no doubt to compliment her more than a round of applause could do.

Mr. Sydney came up next to Harry and murmured, "The Fletchers and the Stilwells are friends, I think?"

"Yes," Harry replied. "We've known Sir Gerald for some time. He and my father would consult on estate matters. I've known all the Stilwell daughters since we were children."

Mr. Sydney nodded as he regarded Gussie at the other end of the room. "Not as pretty as the elder sister, but not a bad looking girl either. Odd kick in her gallop if you ask me, though. Meaning no offense, of course."

It would have been perfectly natural for a man to take umbrage at this description of his friend. But Harry only looked at Gussie with a small smile playing on his lips before making his way over to her. "Odd kick indeed."

***

Gussie accepted the applause for her song with the outward appearance of confidence but was, in fact, internally replaying every fault and mistake she'd made as she played. It had sounded just awful to her ears, but to stop playing from embarrassment would have been worse, so she'd kept on until the song was done. She could escape and recover herself in another room while the other ladies played.

Rising from the stool to do just that, she was confronted by Amy Fletcher. Amy's smile engulfed her entire face. "Miss Stilwell, that was the most beautiful thing I have ever heard. You play so wonderfully! Thank you."

Gussie quickly calculated whether it was worth it to assure Amy that she was dead wrong but decided against it. "Thank you. Though it has been a long time since I have played."

"I wish I could play as well as you. Mama says she will take us up to London in the spring."

Out of the corner of her eye Gussie saw Harry coming their way. "Indeed? That is the place to go. There are many, many music masters there."

Amy nodded with enthusiasm just as Harry stepped up next to her. "Brother, wasn't she simply wonderful? I'm going to play like that someday."

"If you take it as seriously as Gussie has, then you shall, puppet." Harry turned his eyes to Gussie, a joke laughing in them. "Well done."

Though Gussie was sure Amy's praise was sincere, her enthusiasm was taking it rather too far. Still, she wasn't impervious to the Fletchers' compliments. Putting her critical feelings aside for the moment, she bowed her head. "Thank you."

She moved to the side of the room where the door was, accepting compliments from several guests along the way. She didn't realize that Harry was following her until she heard his voice right behind her. "Shall I get you some tea?"

She whirled around, surprised at how close he was but she only wanted to leave the room. "No thank you. Excuse me. I won't be a minute."

She didn't wait to see his reaction but turned and walked herself calmly but resolutely out of the room. She ducked into the doorway of the small parlor just next to the drawing room, closed her eyes and took a deep breath.

So Amy and Harry and the others had said her music was good. What could they know about it? Did they not see all the mistakes in notes and rhythm she'd had to recover from? A flash of anger at Harry for getting her into this mess came over her. Why couldn't he have kept his tongue?

Gussie knew these feelings would eventually pass, but the disappointment in herself was proving difficult to conquer, as it always was. Her sisters had always said she was too hard on herself when she made mistakes, but they never had any advice on how to overcome such criticalness. She took another deep breath. A few more and she could go back into the room with her regular composure before the dancing began.

"What's the matter, Gus?"

She turned to see Harry standing behind her holding a cup of tea in a saucer. "Nothing," she said. "I only needed a moment to myself."

"Liar."

A look of understanding spread across his face as he stepped up to her holding out the tea. "Something's put you out, but you'll have to tell me what it is. It's always the thing that I never guess, and then you become even angrier because of my ineptitude and I'm not about to get into that kind of roundaboutation with you. So, what is it?"

He remembered so many things about her. It felt good to have someone other than Rosy who knew her so well and who sincerely wished to make her feel better. As Harry loomed over her with his great height, she felt he could shield her from anything she wished to hide from, with his face set in a determined, handsome glare that would declare to anyone who saw it that no one distressed Gussie Stilwell under his watch. Then he would turn back to her, his eyes softening, leaning in...

She gave herself an internal shake. She was still angry at him. "My performance was horrid, that's all. Thank you for putting me into such an embarrassing position."

Harry's brows contracted. "Horrid? What do you mean?"

"I haven't played the harp in months. How do you think I sounded? It was awful."

"I didn't hear anything awful. I thought it was very good."

"You're not musical, how would you know what's good?"

"Now look here," he said, frustration creeping into his voice. "I may not play anything, but I know what sounds good and what sounds horrible. You don't think any of the women back in India played music?

Believe me, there are plenty of harps and pianofortes among the Nabobs there. I know what sounds good, thank you very much."

The mention of music in India brought one of Harry's letters to mind. "But you prefer the sitar, don't you?" she asked.

Harry's eyes narrowed as he stared at her. He sniffed and shook his head. "An abrupt change of subject, but yes. Did I tell you that? I'd forgotten."

Gussie nodded. "Two or three years ago. You said the first time you heard it, you thought it was outlandish, but then you grew fond of it."

"I did." He handed her the tea. "You should drink that before it gets cold. Yes, the sitar was beautiful. As was your song just now."

"No, it wasn't. It was horrible. I made so many mistakes. And now that everyone remembers I play the harp, they're going to keep asking me." She looked up accusingly at him.

"Gussie," Harry said, rolling his eyes and raking and hand through his hair. "Could you just stop, for one minute?"

The sharpness in his voice caused Gussie's retort to freeze on her tongue. It had been a juvenile thing to say. She hadn't meant to anger him but couldn't check herself in time.

They didn't speak for a moment or two, neither did they meet the other's eye. At last, Harry said, "You're too clever for your own good sometimes, you know that, Gus? You think you know everything before everyone else and that they couldn't possibly be right about something you've already made up your mind about. But really, just this once, could you believe me, and the others back in there, that your music was lovely to listen to? It's such a small thing when you think about it."

Gussie looked down and took her lips in between her teeth. She wasn't convinced that her playing wasn't poor, but she did know when an apology was in order. "I'm sorry, Harry."

Harry placed a curled finger under her chin and lifted her face up, inclining his own to catch her eye. "I'm sorry too. You're not angry with me anymore? You'll still dance with me?"

"*You're* still angry with *me*."

"No," he assured her, putting his hand down. "It's my own fault. You'd think after all our letters, I'd remember how stubborn you are when you've made up your mind."

It warmed Gussie's heart to think that their letters might have been just as important to his comfort as they had been to hers for all their years apart. She gave a small smile and attempted to lighten the air between them. "I'll know you're still angry with me if you step on my toes more than once."

It worked. Harry glared mischief at her. "Then you'd better be on your guard, Gussie Stilwell."

Gussie narrowed her eyes in return and lifted a brow that was meant to intimidate, as if Harry could be intimidated by her after four years in the jungles of India, but she did it just the same. She was about to say something equally menacing until she realized that Harry's gaze had trailed down her face and was now resting on her lips.

"Harry! There you are."

Mrs. Fletcher's voice behind them jerked Harry's head up. Gussie stayed where she was and looked past Harry to Mrs. Fletcher crossing the hall. "Is everything alright? Why are you two out here?" Mrs. Fletcher asked.

Harry turned to face his mother. "Perfectly fine, ma'am. Gussie needed a breath of cooler air after her exertions at the harp. I was just bringing her some refreshment."

Gussie stared at Harry's back, affronted at his words. Exertion at the harp? She was no weakling. Although, she *had* made a bit of a fuss about the whole ordeal. Perhaps she shouldn't be too offended by his words.

Mrs. Fletcher looked over to Gussie with some concern in her eye. "You are not feeling faint, Gussie, are you?"

Gussie shook her head. "No, ma'am. Not at all."

"Good. That would be a pity. But indeed, you really shouldn't be out here alone, the two of you. You are not children anymore." She turned her attention to Harry. "Come back in, will you? Miss Blackwell is about to sing. She has such a lovely voice. You must hear her."

"Yes, we'll be right in." He held his arm out to Gussie. "Ready?"

A firm supporter of holding one's saucer with two hands whenever possible, Gussie lifted it up to show she couldn't spare an arm. Harry understood at once and offered his other arm to his mother and the three of them walked back to the drawing room.

Before they reached it, Gussie finally brought the teacup to her lips and drank. "It's cold," she murmured to him.

"Your fault," he whispered back.

Once in the drawing room, they parted ways. Gussie placed her tepid tea on a table and returned to Rosy's side.

"You left in a hurry. Are you well?" Rosy asked.

"Fine," Gussie replied, which was true enough, if she didn't think too much about that look in Harry's eye before Mrs. Fletcher interrupted them. It had made her stomach do the most astonishing somersaults.

"I know you hate it, but you did very well," Rosy murmured. "Half the men here couldn't take their eyes off you, including Harry. Didn't you notice?"

"No." When Rosy continued to stare at her, Gussie looked confusion at her. "What?"

Rosy sighed as if defeated and turned her attention to Amelia Blackwell. "Nothing."

Chapter Eleven

May 1813

...I got to witness a baraat today. The groom came in on an elephant decked in silks and finery. You wouldn't believe the procession following him. Such dancing and costumes that I can't do it justice on paper. It makes our English weddings seem somber, dull affairs...

Mrs. Fletcher favored Amelia Blackwell over the other ladies as the candidate for the new Lady Fletcher, as far as Harry could tell. There could be no doubt that Amelia was charming and knew how to engage her audience with her voice as she sang her aria.

Most men would agree that she was the most beautiful girl in the room if one favored fair hair and eyes. Harry was so used to being surrounded by the darker features of the natives of India that, indeed, Amelia was striking. Her father was well off, too. A match between them would almost certainly be prosperous in many ways, if only Harry could be sure he wouldn't be thinking about Gussie after he made his vows.

Amelia finished her song and graciously accepted the applause that followed. It was well deserved, and she didn't seem to be in a hurry to make room for the next girl.

Harry caught his mother looking at him. She lifted her brows in a speculative way that Harry hoped no one else noticed.

After the last of the musical numbers, the servants were called in to roll away the carpets for the dancing. Two fiddlers, a man with a flute, and another with an oboe were brought in and began tuning their instruments as couples came together and formed into sets.

Harry made his way over to where Gussie stood with Rosy, her back to him as they talked. In doing so, he realized that he had sat still for too long. His legs had stiffened from his riding this morning. Now dancing would come at a cost until they loosened up.

A few steps from her, Harry's eyes caught a movement down by Gussie's side. Her fingers were rolling a small fold of her dress back and forth between them. A warm glow of nostalgia spread through him. How could Gussie have changed so much and yet not at all?

She had done that as a child whenever something made her nervous. Why was she nervous now? Was the room too crowded? Was she still overanalyzing her performance on the harp? She couldn't be nervous about dancing with him, could she?

The only answer to the questions in his head was a desire to comfort her, make her feel safe. And there was only one way he knew how to do that just now. Coming up to her, his hand closed around her fidgeting fingers and held her hand fast in a firm but soft hold.

Everything will be all right, Gus, I've got you...

Gussie immediately turned to see who had touched her. He felt her try to jerk her hand away, but he held on. "It's only me, Gus," he murmured.

The alarm on her face flew away as her eyes alighted on Harry's. Her voice came out in a breathy tone. "Harry, you startled me."

"I'm sorry. I'm saying sorry to you a lot tonight, aren't I?"

She tilted her head to the side in acknowledgement, an apologetic look in her eye. "We both are."

Harry felt that warm feeling of 'home' spread through his whole frame at her response. It gave him a warm, heady feeling, almost like what a glass of strong whiskey might do. He wanted to feel like this all the time, and how he wished Gussie might feel it too, someday.

He nodded, then lifted their hands in invitation. "Shall we? And Rosy, you're next, mind."

Rosy scoffed. "You're too late for that. I'm already engaged for the first four dances. You shall have to wait." Her first partner coming up just then, she threw a smile at her two friends before taking the gentleman's hand and following him to the sets that were forming.

Harry waved her off with an irritated hand. While he and Gussie walked to their places, he murmured into her ear. "Still angry with me?"

Gussie shook her head. "Still angry with me?"

He shook his own in return. "No. Let's have a little fun now, why don't we?"

The music began and Gussie answered him with an elegant curtsy. "As you wish, Sir Harry."

Harry grinned and bowed in return. As he came up, he caught a glimpse of his mother behind Gussie standing against the wall with some friends. One of the women pointed her fan in Gussie's direction as she murmured something to Mrs. Fletcher, who did not look pleased. He squinted an eye in thought for a quick moment. If he really went and tried for Gussie, he would need to convince not one, but *two* women that it was indeed a capital idea. But at this moment, as he danced a lively Scottish reel with her, Gussie's company was all he wanted.

If he let his heart run away with him, he would present his suit here and now in the middle of the room, asking her to give him a chance to change her mind about marriage. But one couldn't pounce things upon Gussie. She hated surprises. She had mentioned that time and again in her letters, and Harry had had plenty of personal experience himself. Though he didn't know many girls who would *like* to have a freshly caught fish thrown at them without any warning. Rosy had fumed at him for hours over that incident, but Gussie had not come near him for over a week.

"Are you feeling the effects of all our morning rides?" Gussie asked as they waited their turn to go down the line.

He winced, for one of his sore legs had given out on him a moment before. "That obvious, is it?"

Gussie lifted a shoulder. "A bit. You should keep dancing for the rest of the night. You won't feel so stiff for so long."

Harry bowed his head. "As *you* wish, Miss Stilwell."

As he took her hands to go down the line with her, he studied her face for a moment. Her usual expression, which was something in between stern and distracted, had shifted into a pleasant look of enjoyment. Was it because she enjoyed the dancing, or because she was dancing with him? He would have to keep an eye on her throughout the rest of the evening to see if he could tell.

He would take her advice as well and dance as much as he could. Partly for his stiff body (for Gussie was rarely wrong), and partly to fulfill his promise to his mother to get to know as many young ladies as he could before making his decision and offer for one of them at the Camrose ball in a month's time.

The dance ended, the players finishing their last notes with a flourish. Applauding the musicians, Harry then took Gussie's hand and led her off the floor.

"Well done, Harry," she said. "Not a misstep to be had."

"I told you I wasn't angry at you," he softly replied. He squeezed her hand a little and caught himself just in time to stop him from bringing her hand to his lips to press a kiss on it. He swallowed, trying to wet his suddenly dry mouth. That had been close.

"Then I padded my shoes for nothing, it seems," Gussie said as they reached the edge of the room.

Harry scoffed. "You did not."

"I did. See?"

She shifted her silk gown away from her feet and sure enough, the tips of two handkerchiefs could be seen peeping out of her slippers. Harry couldn't help himself. He let out a booming laugh that rose above the general din of the room. Several heads turned to see what the commotion was about, staring at him with wide eyes. He lifted a hand in apology to those around him and looked at Gussie with a glare. "Now everyone thinks I'm mad. Thank you."

Gussie's eyes held almost as much laughter as he had let out. "It is not my fault that you laugh at the slightest things."

He shot another good-natured glare at her. "Are you thirsty? I'll get you some lemonade or whatever they're serving."

Gussie nodded. "Thank you. Who do you dance with after me?"

"I don't know yet," he said with a shrug. "You're the only one I made sure to ask beforehand."

Gussie looked at him intently as if trying to decide whether he meant it or not. He only smiled before turning to walk to the refreshment table. That remark may have been too much too soon, but before he brought up the idea of a more serious relationship between them, he wanted to get a hint about how Gussie felt toward him without hovering an old promise over her head.

Harry passed Sir Gerald Stilwell on his way to the refreshments. "Sir Harry, my lad," he said jovially, a glass of wine in his hand. "Care for some cards? We're in need of another man."

"Later, perhaps," Harry returned.

Sir Gerald threw him a knowing smile. "Can't pull yourself away from the ladies, is that it? Can't say I blame you. I saw you dancing with my Gussie just now. That's quite a feat. She doesn't dance with just anyone. Will go for weeks at a time without the slightest desire for it. But you always were a favorite of hers. I suppose that hasn't changed."

Sir Gerald lifted his glass in parting before making his way to the card room. Harry stared at his back before recollecting himself and taking a glass of lemonade. A smile played under his mustache. That had been a heartening exchange.

Before he got back to Gussie, Mrs. Fletcher came up to him with Amelia Blackwell beside her. "Harry, I have been talking with Miss Blackwell. She and her mama are to come to tea and, you'll forgive me,

I have said that you would be delighted to take her for a drive around the park if the day is fair. Do say you will."

Harry looked from one expectant face to the other. "Oh. Of course, I *would* be delighted to, Miss Blackwell. And I'll even dare ask, though I think it impossible...are you engaged for the next two dances?"

Amelia's face flushed demurely as she lowered her eyes. "I am not, Sir Harry."

"Well, you are now, if you like. Excuse me while I take this to Gus—Miss Stilwell."

Amelia and Mrs. Fletcher let him pass and he returned to Gussie's side. "Here you are. Are you dancing the next?"

Gussie shook her head before putting her lips to the glass. "Are you? You should, you know."

"Yes, with Miss Blackwell."

Gussie's eyes narrowed but she couldn't reply until she had swallowed her lemonade. "Are you? She is thought to be a good dancer. She was always one of the best at school."

"If she dances as well as she sings, we shall get on famously," he said. "I must go."

He gave a parting nod of the head before walking back to Amelia and taking her into the set just as the music began.

"I thought you had forgotten me," she said, a teasing expression of hurt on her face.

"No such thing," Harry returned.

The dance began, and while they went through the figures with the other couple of their set, there was little time for talking. Amelia danced with grace and perfection, and while they could not say more than a word or two to each other as they moved, she was very attentive to him in the looks and smiles she gave him. She was a taking young lady, and Harry didn't think it would take much on his part to make any suit from him agreeable to her. She would receive a title, and Camrose, though it had its fair share of debts, was a prosperous estate, all things considered.

He caught sight of Gussie over Amelia's shoulder speaking with another guest and wondered what she would say if he asked her for another dance. At a large public assembly, they could probably get away with it, being such old friends. But this was a small, private dance where everyone knew everyone. He wouldn't press his luck. Besides, she would probably say no.

***

Gussie danced here and there with anyone who might ask her, but most of the time she was sitting and doing one of the things she liked best when in a room full of people. She took to studying the guests and trying to guess what they might be thinking based on their expressions and reactions to those around them.

She watched several people. Mary, who despite being so quiet and unassuming, danced almost as much as Rosy, who was never without a partner. Mrs. Barrett looked pleased as Harry took her daughter out onto the floor. She still had hopes of something coming from that, it seemed. Mrs. Fletcher looked on Harry and her daughters with what looked like maternal pleasure, but there was a certain strain in her eye that made Gussie wonder what might be worrying her so.

And of course, she watched Harry.

Like Rosy, he danced every dance with a gaiety that was infectious to anyone around him. Gussie wondered at people who loved company so much. He seemed to grow brighter and happier with each passing hour, which baffled Gussie, who couldn't wait until Mr. and Mrs. Barrett deemed it time to call for their carriage to take them back to Broadstone. But that was the problem with having a friend who loved to dance. Rosy would stay until dawn dancing, if she could. She would cause such a ruckus in London, if her parents would ever take her.

Harry talked and laughed with all his partners with such ease, caus-ing them to smile at the least thing he said. In fact, he had only to look at his partners and several of them would blush and smile, half in love with him already, Gussie was sure. She pursed her lips. She sup-posed they couldn't help themselves. Harry had everything to recom-mend himself to anyone he chose: a title, a prosperous estate, an easy-going manner, and good looks to boot.

Yes, such a handsome man. There were plenty of handsome men of her acquaintance in London, but she fully admitted to herself that she liked being with this one best. Liked looking at him too. It did not escape her notice that many other ladies in the room, young and old, looked to be of like mind.

As the clock struck eleven, Gussie could see that Harry, for all his love of people, was ready for the night to be over. Despite his constant movement, she was sure that he needed a rest after the ceaseless riding and hunting of the past week. Guests were starting to take leave of their hosts, but Gussie saw Squire Barrett and her father with their heads together, doubtless talking about the logistics of the next hunt. They might be at it for a while. She looked back over to where Harry was, still surrounded by a few of his partners.

If the desire to speak to him again before she left were any less, she wouldn't brave coming up to a group of girls she did not care for and who did not much care for her in return. But the pull to be near him again was as strong as it was sudden. Still, she could not bring herself to join the group and so waited on a nearby chair with her cloak in her lap.

Amelia Blackwell was the most talkative of the girls. That wasn't surprising—she had been a miniature matriarch of the pack of girls at school. Back then, the other girls would gaggle after her wherever she went and agree with whatever she said. She'd had that way about her. At one point Amelia cast a glance Gussie's way before turning back to Harry. A moment later the words, "we are *very* particular about who we invite to our private balls," came to her ears along with another sharp look from Amelia.

Gussie was too tired to dissect this verbal barb. It bounced off her fatigue and fell harmlessly to the floor. She might pick it up and inspect it later, when she was rested, but the thought of trying to interpret the thoughts and motives of Amelia Blackwell held no real interest for her.

Eventually, the rest of the families gathered themselves and left for the night. Mr. Welbeck had joined Mr. Barrett and Sir Gerald, so the rest of the Barrett party must wait a little longer.

Gussie watched Harry say a final farewell to Amelia as she stepped outside to her carriage. He then let out a great sigh and leaned against the wall, nearly upsetting a painting behind him. He shot out a quick hand to stop it from falling and looked around himself with alarm.

"I saw that," Gussie said from across the room.

"Then tell no one," he replied. He walked over to her and put out a hand as if to test the wall for a secure position before leaning against it. "That's better. What a night. I could march and drill all day long before dancing and gaming half the night away, and I still didn't feel as pulled as I do now."

Gussie leaned her head against the wall next to him. As she did, her eyes grew heavy. "You grow accustomed to a certain kind of exertion, I suppose, but when another kind comes along, you have to start all over again."

Harry grunted in response and with his head pressed against the wall turned to look down at her. "You wouldn't have said no to leaving two hours ago, I think. How long will you stay up reading before you sleep?"

Gussie raised her brows as if to shrug. It took less energy than lifting her shoulders. "Until my thoughts let me."

"And what do you think about?"

Where to begin? How much she had enjoyed her time with him? How he was not only amusing, but handsome as well? How the Pact was still on her mind, even though he had released her? No. "Oh, things."

Harry didn't reply but rubbed his face with a heavy hand and heaved out another sigh. Gussie frowned, picking up on his mood. This wasn't just fatigue. "What is the matter?"

"It's a lot to take in, this." He waved a vague hand in the air.

"But you liked it. You enjoyed yourself tonight, that was obvious."

"I did. That doesn't mean...did you watch me all night?" he asked, a teasing tone coming into his voice.

Gussie swallowed and hurried to assure him (and perhaps herself) that he was not *that* important to her. "I watch everyone around me, you know that. Go on. It doesn't mean what?"

Harry eyed her but continued. "That doesn't mean it shouldn't have been John dancing all night instead of me."

The mention of his dead brother laid a heavy air on them both. They were silent for a moment before Gussie ventured, "But he would want you to enjoy it, since you are here and he isn't. Wouldn't he?"

Harry huffed silently. "You're right. As usual. I'm not fit to be a baronet, Gus. I never was. I was never trained for it. Neither was John, but he could always take up anything as if it were nothing. He could have taken Camrose in hand and wouldn't be making a mess of things and asking the same questions over and over enough to make my steward want to pull his hair out—and mine, I imagine."

"But you are taking things in hand. Camrose isn't in ruins."

"Not yet," he said pessimistically. He bowed his head down. "And I need to find a wife. Soon."

Gussie raised open eyes to him, but he continued staring at the floor. "Soon? How soon?"

"Engaged before new year, soon. Married before the spring, soon. Before I die in some quick and unexpected way...soon."

Gussie looked straight ahead of her, her mind in a frenzy as she processed what he had just said. She didn't have years until Harry married and changed everything—she had mere weeks. Why had she not thought of this before? It made complete sense. Two healthy baronets of Camrose had died before him (his brother, John, not even realizing he was a baronet), all without heirs. "Are you afraid you'll die?" she asked.

He shook his head. "No. I have no such fear, but my mother...I promised her."

Gussie nodded slowly as she took in his words. Mrs. Fletcher had already lost one son. She was such an openly loving woman, always showering her children with praises and affection. Gussie could never understand people like her. It wasn't that Gussie could not love. She loved a great deal. But she could not pet and croon and make much of her loved ones the way some women could. If Mrs. Fletcher had so much love for her children, perhaps in her grief she was afraid of losing another.

"How will you find her?" she asked, her voice subdued.

Harry shrugged. "By dancing and driving with every girl in the county, I suppose."

Including me? Gussie wondered before she could dash away the words from her mind.

"Any advice on how to choose a bride?"

Gussie looked at him. "What?"

Harry grinned with one side of his mouth, causing half of his mustache to skew upward. "Have you read any books about how to choose a bride in only a few weeks?"

Gussie let out a breath of laughter. She had never come across what Plato or Newton thought about the matter. "Perhaps in a novel? Only I've never read one. I'm sorry, I can't help you."

Harry sighed. "It's just as well. I can only hope she will not think me mad for proposing so soon, whomever she may be."

"Yes, heaven help her."

Harry shifted his position against the wall, folding his arms. "I think I'd make an excellent husband, admit it. Well, as much as a hulking bull calf like me can be. At least she wouldn't have to put up with much of anything. I am excessively easy to please. I only ask that she hire a good cook."

Gussie's lips twitched, but she lowered a disbelieving brow. "She would likely be driven mad because you can't take anything seriously."

He smiled and shrugged. "Maybe so, but that's nothing to signify. Well, what I mean is, it would be a small annoyance. *You* would not mind my cockamamie ways, if we married, would you? We'd get along quite well, I'm sure. *I'd* enjoy it, at all events."

What had he just said?

Gussie tried to register his words, but her mind felt frozen in place.

"What?" she said in the barest whisper.

They had already agreed to let the Pact stay in the past. That was what had happened in the drawing room before dinner, wasn't it? Had he been talking about something else? No, that was impossible, what else could they have been speaking of? Her thoughts spun so fast that they melted the ice that held her in place. She rose from her chair and wrapped her cloak around her. "I am never marrying, Harry. You know that."

Harry pushed his shoulder off the wall, surprise in his face. "It was only a joke, Gussie. I didn't mean anything by it, but..."

"Don't say another word, please," she said, almost hissing.

Before he could respond, Rosy and Mrs. Barrett came up to them. "Come along, Gussie, the carriage is here." She turned to Harry. "Rosy tells me she'll have the pleasure of riding with you again this week. I charge you to bring her back safe to me."

Mrs. Barrett, her eyes merry, pointed a strict finger at him while Rosy looked at her mother with some annoyance.

Harry's eyes darted to Gussie once more before replying to Mrs. Barrett's teasing. Gussie didn't hear what he said. Her head was swimming with the things she had discovered in the last few moments.

Harry and his family were afraid of him dying before having children. He needed to marry and had to choose a bride sooner rather than later. She didn't have the years of comfortable friendship with him that she thought she would have. No matter whom his wife would be, she and Harry wouldn't be able to be friends with the freedom they enjoyed now. She was certain, in every bone of her body, that she would lose him.

Gussie was aware that she followed the Barretts out the door and into their carriage, but it was as if she were only an observer and not a participant in the action. Something had happened inside her when Harry had told her he would enjoy being married to her. Some force, some sensation, kept twisting and pulling and squeezing her heart. Something had fallen out of place, or was it trying to make room for itself? Harry 'wouldn't mind' being married to her.

That begged the question, would she truly 'mind' being married to him?

Chapter Twelve

November 1813

> *...I was at Hatchards bookshop before we came to Oakleigh for the shooting, and what do you think I found? It is called the European in India, by a Captain Williamson. Do you know him? I shall read it from start to finish and write my findings to you. You may tell me if they are accurate or not...*

Harry grimaced as he felt his horse flinch underneath him. In his anxiety to get to Rosy and Gussie as quickly as possible, he had put the spur on too hard. He gave the gray a pat as they trotted out of Camrose and onto the lane. "Sorry, old boy."

It was two days after the Welbeck's party, two days since he had seen Gussie. It had also been two days since he had ridden, and every movement his horse made beneath him had him bracing himself against the soreness in his legs. They would warm up to the motion, but he was glad he had cried off from the hunt Sir Gerald Stilwell was hosting at Oakleigh the next day. He'd claimed he had estate business to see to, which was true enough. There might never be an end to the things he was learning and had yet to learn about keeping Camrose.

During those forty-eight hours, Harry had replayed again and again in his mind the moment his joke had turned disastrous. There were plenty of times that his glib tongue and lightheartedness had run away with him, but rarely had he cursed himself more for being so careless as he'd been in this instance. Had she really meant what she had said? She really would never marry? She must have, for he had never known Gussie to say something she didn't mean.

Harry had known this almost as long as he'd known her, but ever since John's death, when he'd begun to read and reread her letters to the point where he knew many of them by heart, he had always hoped in the back of his mind that he would somehow be able to change her mind. That his loving her would be enough to make marriage an attractive thing.

Obviously, that had not been the case last night. His decision to imply that the Pact should be marked down as fanciful childhood play had felt like the right thing to do; Gussie's response indicated that. And he was so pleased with himself. What must he do? Bring up the idea of marriage to her with a devil-may-care attitude before she had time to blink. He had his reward. The slightest touch on the subject had made her double down on her position.

Harry let out a great sigh and shook his head in frustration. He had rushed her. One couldn't sneak up on Gussie Stilwell and pounce, especially with something like that. He'd known this for years, and still the enthusiasm of discovering he loved her and seeing her again after only having had her letters for so long had gotten the better of him. He'd had five months on a ship to fall in love with her letters as they kept him company.

She had only found out about his inheritance and return barely four weeks ago. He may have read their correspondence over and over again, but it didn't follow that she had done the same. He needed to see her again and make up any ground he'd lost.

He spotted Gussie far up the lane coming from Broadstone with Rosy. The day was overcast, and behind them darker clouds were gathering which would surely bring rain. It was time to see what damage to their relationship he had inflicted. He lifted his hat and hailed them. They had their heads together. Rosy was telling Gussie something of great importance, it seemed. At his greeting, Rosy shot her hand up and gave it an enthusiastic wave in return. Gussie only lifted her head in a nod as they drew closer. Harry huffed out a laugh. Two friends so opposite from each other you'd be hard put to find.

After waving to him, Rosy's head went straight back to Gussie's to finish whatever she was saying. As they drew nearer, he caught the whispered words 'don't know what is in Mama's head...couldn't marry him if my life depended on it!'

Laughter bubbled up inside Harry. If Mrs. Barrett's recent attentions were any indication, he had an idea of who Rosy was talking about. The feeling was mutual. "Good morning," he called out.

"Good morning, Harry," Rosy returned.

"That's *Sir* Harry to you, you rattle pate. Won't you ever mind your manners?" he said, unable to stop himself from getting a rise out of her.

Rosy rolled her eyes. "You'll always be just little old Harry Fletcher to me, even if you were to inherit a dukedom."

"Thank you for always being there to keep me humble."

"I'm only here to irritate you. Gussie keeps you humble," Rosy said, laughing at her joke while Gussie cast her a stern glance.

Wasn't that the truth?

If Harry had his way, and if he knew it was the right way, he would send Rosy on ahead so he could speak to Gussie right away. But given that she had only made eye contact with him once, he felt it best to go on with the ride as if nothing had happened. Like the time he had thrown the fish at her, perhaps Gussie needed time to come around again. He would let her come to him, and when she did, well, he would cross that bridge when he came to it.

"Shall we?" he asked.

They chose to hack along the lanes and fields surrounding the village of Ryhall. Rosy kept the conversation mostly on horses and how excited she was about the next crop of foals coming that spring. "Our stallion, Dedlock, doesn't have an equal in any of the Shires. His lines run through Gimcrack and the Godolphin, you know. Papa raised him up himself."

Harry went along with her enthusiasm. It was hard not to catch onto her excitement and reply in kind. But all the while, he stole furtive looks at Gussie to try to gauge what she might be thinking about.

It was a futile effort. One could never tell what was going on in that head of hers. As a game, he had asked her plenty of times when they were young, for her answers were always so outlandish: "Trying to sort out Kepler's laws on planetary motion; Hypatia should have been made a member of the Library of Alexandria too, I think; if Egyptians were all buried in pyramids, shouldn't there be more of them than those three big ones?"

Upon coming up to the edge of the village itself, the heavenly scent of hot buns from the bakery filled Harry's senses. He wasn't the only one. Rosy inhaled deeply. "Oh, that breakfast wasn't still so far away."

Instantly, Harry urged his horse onto the main street, turned back his head, and grinned. "Come on, then."

"Oh, Harry, thank you," cried Rosy at the same time Gussie murmured, "Oh, Harry, no..."

Five minutes later saw them all munching on gingerbread still warm from the oven with Harry wondering if he had done right in insisting on the treat. Gussie had been quiet before, but a sudden awkwardness had cropped up between them now, and he was second-guessing himself. What did he do now?

Rosy eyed the sky. The darker clouds that had been gathering in the west were almost overhead. "We shouldn't stand too long here. I don't want Silvertail getting wet. Me neither, for that matter. It's too cold."

Harry and Gussie nodded in agreement but said nothing. Rosy looked between the two of them, pursing her lips. Harry only met her eye once before he looked down to break a piece of his gingerbread off and pop it into his mouth. She had that calculating look in her eye. He had better shake off this ticklish muteness that had come over him and say something to make them laugh before she started getting curious.

Rosy studied her last bit of gingerbread a moment before offering it to her horse. "You've been quiet today, Gussie. What book kept you up all night this time? Harry, did you know that she brings her very own supply of candles so that my father won't be burdened with the cost of it? Isn't that thoughtful of her?"

"It is," Harry replied, looking at Gussie.

Gussie didn't raise her head from her gingerbread. "It's the obvious thing to do. I use so many."

A scowl settled on Rosy's brow, but she looked to Harry next. "Have you heard from that family you became friends with on the ship? You said they promised to visit soon, did you not?"

"The Fentons. I haven't. I did invite them for Christmas, but I do not expect to hear from them until the spring, if they write back at all."

Harry heard the soft plop of a drop of rain hit his hat. Then another. The girls noticed it right away too.

"We'd better head back," he said. Shoving the rest of the gingerbread into his mouth, he motioned the girls to their horses. He first threw Gussie, then Rosy into their saddles before mounting his gray.

The raindrops came down faster and Harry knew it wouldn't be long before the downpour would come out of hiding in the clouds. "We'll be drenched through before we make it back to Broadstone. Camrose is closer. Come with me there and wait it out."

Camrose Hall lay two miles from Ryhall. By the time they came into the courtyard of the stables at the back of the house, not only had the downpour begun, but the wind had picked up, chilling them all to the bone. Two grooms came running out of the stables to meet them, grabbing the bridles of the girls' horses while Harry helped them dismount. A footman with an umbrella appeared, and Gussie and Rosy huddled underneath it on their way to the house with Harry close behind.

"My," said Mrs. Fletcher when she got to them in the hall. "Thank goodness nothing happened to you. Come into my little room and straight to the fire, my dears."

"It was only a little rain, Mama," Harry said, praying that his teeth wouldn't start chattering in front of her. Would he ever get used to the cold again? He turned to the footmen who had taken their hats and gloves. "Two more covers for breakfast. That rain isn't stopping any-time soon."

"Of course, you must stay until it has stopped and you are quite dry," Mrs. Fletcher said.

Amy and Charlotte were delighted to have two surprise guests join-ing them at the breakfast table and made the meal lively. Once they had eaten their fill, both sisters begged to cry off from their morning lessons.

"It would be rude of us as hosts when we have guests," Charlotte reasoned. "May we please show them what we have found in the attics instead? At least until it stops raining? Miss Barrett, we found the most delightful clothes to play in. We are up there almost every day."

"It may rain all day, for all I know," Mrs. Fletcher replied, but there was no bite in her voice, and she said they may if it pleased Rosy and Gussie.

Rosy agreed immediately to the adventure, but Gussie said, "You will excuse me, if you please. I'd rather explore the library instead, if I may?"

Harry could see that his mother didn't take Gussie's seeming disin-terest in her daughters well, but the permission was granted.

"I'll take you there," he said.

Before Gussie could reply to his invitation, Mrs. Fletcher said, "Surely that isn't necessary. Miss Stilwell knows all too well where the library is. I would rather you go up with the girls, they might need you."

"Yes, Harry, come up with us," his sisters cried.

"Do go up with them," Gussie said. "I don't need any assistance."

Harry had a feeling that she was deliberately trying to avoid his company, but there was nothing he could do when everyone in the room wanted him in the attics and not the library. "Very well, lead the way," he replied.

Chapter Thirteen

You may find this difficult to believe, but English rain is noth-ing compared to the monsoon months I am enduring. Soldiers who have been here longer than John and I say it will last until October. One is never dry, for when it stops raining, the air is so damp that you stay wet until the next downpour hits. I believe I would have fared better on the Peninsula braving Napoleon's armies. What do you think? Shall I put in for a transfer?...

Rain sang a staccato melody against the windows of the library as Gussie walked up and down the length of the long oak bookcases. Which book might be enticing enough to take her mind off her thoughts surrounding Harry? It was not her reading that had kept her up until the small hours of the morning the past two nights but her worries.

What was she to do about Harry? Her conviction that marriage would hold no attractions nor offer anything she wanted that she did not have already still held, but she could feel cracks forming in her foundation when it came to her friend. Marriage to Harry? That would mean having her friend for life. The thought was a comforting one.

If only she had anything to offer him in return.

Never in her life had she been fearful of her father forcing a hus-band on her. He was far too neglectful for that, and not even Phyllis's ambitions to get all his daughters married off to have the house to her-self had moved him from his comfortable position when it came to Gussie, anyway. In the settlements of her mother's fortune, it stated that any daughters who were unmarried by the time they were thirty would receive a portion of Lady Stilwell's dowry to live on. Gussie had con-vinced her father years ago that once she gained that comfortable inheritance, she would be sure never to burden him again and be perfectly happy in her little country cottage full of books and surrounded by beautiful walks.

But if she ever found herself with no choice but to marry, she would want it to be Harry. Yes, she could do it with Harry.

Probably...possibly?

A voice behind her startled her out of her anxious musings. "Miss Stilwell?"

She turned and found Amy Fletcher standing in the middle of the room, her fingers fiddling with the ends of the pink ribbon tied around her waist. "Hello, Amy," Gussie said.

Amy smiled and fumbled over a greeting. Gussie raised her brows. What was the matter with her?

Amy bit her lip and tried again. "Miss Stilwell, I only wanted to tell you again how lovely your song at the harp was. I love the harp so much and think you are *so* talented that I wondered—"

She began to fumble over her words again before stopping completely, her face blushing crimson. In that moment, she rather reminded Gussie of her sister Mary. So timid and afraid to speak sometimes, especially if it was something important. Gussie guessed Amy was under the same pressure. Whatever it was, it was important. "Thank you, you're very kind. Go on. Wonder what?"

Amy took a deep breath and said in a rush, "I know you love reading and being by yourself and not being bothered by other people, but would you be so kind as to give me a lesson or two on the harp and show me how to play it better, please?"

Gussie would not spend any amount of time near that instrument for anything if she could help it. She moved to speak, but her thoughts must have manifested in her face first, for Amy raised her hands, palms out. "I know I am so much younger than you and that you've never really liked me, but I just had to ask. We cannot go to London until the spring, and I simply cannot wait that long to learn, so...please?"

You've never really liked me.

Amy's words took Gussie aback. She was about to say that it was not true but held back. It was not true, but it was not *not* true either. She held no ill will toward either of Harry's little sisters, she had simply been uninterested in them. She had always thought Amy's overly affectionate and cheerful behaviors odd and had never known a wish to cultivate a friendship with someone like that who was also so much younger than she. It seemed that her disinterest in Amy had been taken by that girl as proof that she did, in fact, dislike her.

You need to be more careful, said a reproving voice in Gussie's head.

She didn't know how to respond to Amy's accusation, but the immediate effect it had on her was the softening of Gussie's heart not to the harp, but to Amy. "I can help you a little." She looked out the window. Still raining. "I am not going anywhere, so why not now?"

Amy's face shone as bright as a sunbeam. "Thank you, Miss Stilwell! Thank you, thank you...I don't know how to thank you!"

She hopped up and down, clapping her hands. Each bounce brought her closer to Gussie, who leaned away. To prevent herself from being smothered by the embrace that was sure to come next, Gussie walked toward the door, beckoning for Amy to follow. "You did just now, so there's that. You've exaggerated my skill horribly, but you won't discover that for yourself until you're more out and about in society. The instrument is still in the drawing room, I take it?"

"Yes, and I play it every day."

The two of them came out of the library and crossed the hall to the drawing room. Once inside, Amy grabbed an upholstered stool, brought it to the harp and sat down, eagerness shining in her eyes.

"Stand up. You'll try in a moment," Gussie said. "If I may?"

***

Harry had never allowed his sisters to drag him up to the attics during their explorations. He always had some sort of business to attend to, as he did now. His steward was expecting him in his study at any minute to discuss the repairs of several of the houses rented out to tenants and farmers on Camrose land.

So he finally broke away from Rosy and Charlotte (Amy had run off not long into their play) and their unholy desires to see him dressed in women's hats and silks from fifty years ago. He stepped down the several staircases on his way to the library to see Gussie one more time. The rain was letting up, and likely she and Rosy would be able to go home before his business was concluded.

When he reached the top of the stairs in the main hall, he found his mother down below, peeking into the drawing room. The faint sound of the harp strings could be heard emanating from the room. His boots fell muffled on the carpet, but they made enough noise for Mrs. Fletcher to turn around. She immediately gestured for him to be quiet and beckoned him to come closer with a wave of her hand.

Intrigued, Harry quieted his movements and crept up to the drawing room door. He could hear a voice coming from inside. What was Gussie doing in there, and to whom was she talking?

"What is it?" he mouthed to his mother.

Mrs. Fletcher put a hand on his arm, a smile lighting her face. She made room for him to look in without being spotted. The sight that met his eyes was not one he would ever have expected.

Gussie was teaching Amy how to play the harp.

Harry exchanged looks with his mother. She mirrored the surprise in his own face. He felt sure that his mother had taken Gussie's apparent snub to Amy too personally, but even he could admit that Gussie had never shown Amy anything beyond common politeness. Yet here she was, showing his sister which fingers to use when plucking three strings at a time on an instrument she despised.

Gussie's instructions were short and to the point, but Amy didn't seem to mind her blunt, no-nonsense manner. That was only Gussie's nature, but Harry knew not everyone appreciated it. His mother included.

Mrs. Fletcher pressed his arm with her hand and motioned for him to back away from the door a few paces with her. "I would never have thought it of her," she said. "She has always disliked both the girls. I wonder how this came about."

Half of Harry's mouth stretched into a smile on hearing this criticism of his friend. "She does have peculiarities and particularities, but if she chooses not to like something or someone, there is a reason for it. I don't think she's ever truly disliked Amy or Charlotte. You do her a disservice, Mama. Were you fond of girls so much younger than you when you were a young woman?"

Mrs. Fletcher opened her mouth to speak but stopped, thinking. "Perhaps not all of them," she said at last. She looked up at him with worry in her eyes. "Do you like her so much, my love?"

Harry knew the answer would disappoint her, but she deserved to know the truth. He put a hand on her arm and gave it a little squeeze. "I do like her so much, my dear."

Mrs. Fletcher pursed her lips and pushed a long breath out of her nose. "And what if she will not have you? She told me herself she has no intention of marrying. I don't care how long you have known each other; I think it would be a foolish thing, to break your heart over her. I do not want to see you hurt so."

Harry motioned for this mother to follow him to the back saloon to continue the conversation. He didn't want to risk anyone (Gussie included) hearing this. Closing the door behind him, he asked, "Is your only real concern that Gussie doesn't like me enough? That she would refuse me if I asked her to be my wife?"

"I don't think she likes anyone enough. All I see her caring for is her solitude and her books."

"Mama, you are wrong," Harry said. "If you only knew. If you only allowed yourself to become more acquainted with her."

It was on the tip of his tongue to tell her about Gussie's letters, but he held it back just in time. While her letters had given him no reason to think she'd written him with an eye to a future marriage, the degree of loyalty they showed to their friendship was nothing short of remarkable. "Believe me when I say, ma'am, that there is more to Gussie Stilwell that meets the eye."

Mrs. Fletcher frowned. "What do you mean? You have done nothing improper, have you?"

"Mama, really." Harry was not of the untruthful sort. Writing letters to an unmarried woman halfway across the world for years on end was most improper, but he was spared trying to come up with a suitable change of subject when not one but two suitable changes walked into the room.

The first was a footman informing him that Pritchard was awaiting his pleasure in the study. A moment later, the second was Amy, bursting into the room with all the force of a whirlwind and running up to Mrs. Fletcher. "Mama, what do you think? Miss Stilwell has been showing me the right way to play the harp. I can play three cords now! And she says my glissando is wretched."

Mrs. Fletcher frowned. "Did she, my darling? Well!"

After Amy's exuberance, Gussie's quieter entrance into the room was like the current of a deep river, calm and steady. "Quite wretched, but that will change once her fingers are strengthened by practice. She will master it in no time if she does not shirk."

Harry couldn't interpret the expression on his mother's face and quickly lifted a hand to ask silence from everyone while he turned to the footman. "Tell Pritchard I will be with him shortly."

The footman dismissed, Amy continued, grabbing both Harry's and Mrs. Fletcher's hands. "And I *will* practice. You both must come and watch me. Come now. Make haste!"

"Of course, I should like to see what you've done," said Mrs. Fletcher, squeezing Amy's shoulders and embracing her.

Amy extricated herself only to take Mrs. Fletcher's hand again to lead her to the door. "Miss Stilwell, will you come to so you can tell me if I am doing it right?"

Gussie shot a glance at Harry, quickly averting her eye when she found him watching her. "Very well," she said.

Amy may or may not have heard her, for she was already halfway out the door with Mrs. Fletcher. As Gussie moved out of the room, Harry fell into step with her. "Thank you for showing her a few things. I haven't seen her so happy in some time, and that is saying something, for she is always happy." He chuckled a little at this, but Gussie only nodded her head. "It was very kind of you. I can't think you enjoyed it much. What made you do it, if I may ask?"

She met his eye for a fleeting moment before looking ahead again. "I never intend to be rude to people, but I think I must have been so to her at some point, and she became a little afraid of me. I am so blunt that sometimes, well...it is something I need to be more careful about. It was not bothersome, as you put it. It did not bother me much at all once we began. Perhaps I like the harp better when I am not the one playing it. Your sister is clever enough. It was nothing, I assure you."

There she went trying to be humble about the use of the extraordinary skills that were, for her, usually so easy to acquire when she put her mind to it. Harry stopped walking, unable to help regarding her with a little wonder. She was a spectacular girl with an earnest heart underneath her curtness. How could he not love her for that? If only other people could see it as easily as he could. If only she would *let* them.

Gussie caught on a step or two later and turned back to him with inquiring eyebrows. His boots falling heavy and slow against the wooden floor, he stepped up to her, willing her to hold his gaze for just a moment more. "Not so, Gus. It meant something to her, and it means something to me too."

And there *he* went looking before he leapt again! If a simple joke about marriage had made her shy away, what would a sincere statement like that do?

He didn't wait to see what her response might be. Feeling that forward motion was the best strategy, he moved forward to the drawing room door. Once inside, he took a seat in the great wingback chair near the hearth, wondering if Gussie would ever talk to him again after his romantic gaffes. He did not look at her as she took her place near Amy to oversee the performance of the three chords.

These were played if not with perfection, certainly with an enthusiasm that made up for the repeated tries until Amy played them clean.

Mrs. Fletcher clapped her hands. "Bravo, darling. With that talent, we must get you up to London and into some proper music lessons as soon as may be." She looked to Gussie and said with some reserve, "Thank you, Miss Stilwell."

Gussie stiffened her shoulders slightly as she bowed her head. "Not at all. I was happy to do it."

"Will you come tomorrow, Miss Stilwell?" Amy asked. "I will have my chords perfected by then, I promise."

Here, Mrs. Fletcher shook her head. "Now, my dear, we must not inconvenience Miss Stilwell any further. Likely she is engaged elsewhere already."

But, likely to the surprise of all three Fletchers, Gussie said, "Not tomorrow, for I am engaged. But I could come the day after, if it would be convenient."

Amy beamed and thanked her profusely. "That will be convenient, won't it, Mama? Harry?"

"Ah, well," Mrs. Fletcher murmured, giving a fleeting glance toward Harry.

He thought he knew the dilemma running through her mind. She knew his inclinations toward Gussie and was not in favor of them. But to refuse Gussie's offer would mean disappointing Amy, which would come close to breaking her tender, motherly heart.

"Surely it is all right with us," he said. "I could bring her back here after our ride, if the weather is in our favor. If not, she could come after breakfast. Would that suit you, Amy? Yes, I thought it would. What do you say, Mama?"

With Amy looking at her with such pleading eyes, what could she say? "We would be delighted, Miss Stilwell," she said at last.

Amy clapped her hands, rose from the stool, and went over to Gussie with outstretched hands. Gussie only hesitated a moment before reaching out and taking them with her own. "Remember," she said, "I am not as good as you think I am, but I can teach you one or two more things."

Voices outside in the hall told the drawing room occupants that Rosy and Charlotte were on their way to them and very soon the whole party was reunited.

"It's stopped raining," Rosy said. "Gussie, we had better get back before they begin to worry."

"Indeed, it is time for us to leave," Gussie agreed.

Harry went and pulled the bell rope. "I will call for your horses to be put to, but I'm afraid I have to say goodbye here. I've left Pritchard waiting longer than I intended, poor fellow."

Chapter Fourteen

August 1812

America has declared war on Great Britain, and they are fighting about it across the ocean. Has word about it reached you yet in Bombay? But one cannot really expect the king to support the Americans trading with our enemy at time like this...

Gussie, with Rosy in tow, came back to Camrose Hall as promised not only once, but thrice during the next week, the last time being joined by Mrs. Barrett for tea with all the Fletchers. Gussie gave Amy enough exercises to practice to last several weeks and found Amy to be an apt pupil, clever and quick to pick up her instructions.

Though she still thought the girl had far too much enthusiasm not only for the harp but for everything in general, Gussie liked and understood her better with each lesson. But she found herself quite exhausted coming away from each time and required long stretches of solitude before she had any desire for company again. Time which she did not get. The hunting and shooting season was in full swing in Rutland. If it wasn't a private party or dinner, it was a public assembly in Ryhall or one of the other surrounding villages. Gussie cried off as much as she dared from these events, but it was still not enough to make her feel rested.

On her visits to Camrose, she sometimes saw Harry. Sometimes not. And when she did, it was only a glimpse of him before he was off to inspect some piece of his property or about to shut himself in his study with his secretary or steward or some other man of business. During these quick interactions, there was nothing in Harry to suggest that he might be thinking of marriage and Gussie in the same breath. He was just Harry, whose object in life was to bring a smile and a laugh to everyone around him and he frequently succeeded.

But in the present moment, when the Barretts and Fletchers were all gathered for some refreshment, Gussie caught his gaze lingering on her more than once out of the corner of her eye. She tried to make nothing of it, but that was difficult when she was looking for every chance to study him back.

The talk during the little repast chiefly surrounded Christmas, only a week away, and Mrs. Fletcher's ball, a fortnight away. Gussie did not take part in the conversation, choosing to take in deep breaths of the coffee Mrs. Fletcher invited them to partake of in place of tea. Harry had brought several pounds of it back from India. She closed her eyes as the earthy aroma gently swirled about her face. The two spoonfuls of sugar she had added to it did little to take away the bitter scent, but she was growing to like it that black.

She had stayed awake far too late in the night not only reading but trying to decipher her feelings surrounding Harry. Combine that with Amy's enthusiastic lesson and a social visit with a room full of people straight after that...she was ready to go home.

"Gussie, are you well?" Rosy next to her asked.

Gussie opened her eyes and gave a small nod. "Perfectly."

Rosy's voice had been quiet, but not quiet enough to escape the notice of Mrs. Barrett. "Is Gussie unwell?" she asked, looking at her with concern. "You do look pale."

Every eye in the room was on Gussie now, not just Harry's. "I am well, I thank you," she assured them.

"Are you sure?" Harry asked.

"But her cheeks are very pink now, aren't they?" Charlotte said.

"Is the fire too hot, I wonder?" Mrs. Fletcher next. "Does anyone else feel it?"

"I am not overheated, I promise you—"

"Amy, fetch her that screen, will you?"

"She's nowhere near the fire, Mama," Harry said, his eyes never leaving Gussie.

This had to stop. Gussie stood up. "A turn about the garden would help, I think. I have been sitting for too long."

Rosy put down her cup and saucer. "I'll come with you."

Not ideal for someone who wished to be alone, but Gussie wouldn't argue.

"I'll come too."

Gussie's heart dropped to her toes, and a rush of heat surged up her neck as Harry rose from his chair and came toward her. She prayed no one would notice her discomfort or if they did, they wouldn't connect it with her confusion about Harry.

"Harry, is that necessary? If Rosy is going with her," Mrs. Fletcher said.

"I will make sure that any guest of mine is well," was Harry's answer.

He offered an arm to Gussie, who slid her hand through and rather stiffly placed it on the crook of his arm. Rosy came to her other side and took hold of her other arm as they walked out the door.

Gussie felt like an invalid, which only made her angry. She was fatigued, yes, but had felt perfectly fine until Harry had come toward her. Now she was indeed feeling a little lightheaded.

Once out of the drawing room, Rosy started on her first. "What is it? I didn't mean to bring everyone's attention to you, but I was worried. You looked so...I don't know. I was worried, that's all."

"What is the matter, Gus?" Harry asked, craning his neck down at her.

Gussie didn't want to tell him that she was tired from coming over to help his sister. After agreeing to come the second time, it had been her idea to come twice more. She was getting used to Amy but wasn't to the point of being able to be in her company so frequently. And she would not, for any consideration, tell him that she could not sleep nights for thinking of him and wondering what a future with him might look like.

So, she went with a reason she knew they would accept without question. "I stayed up too late reading again. Perhaps I should stop."

Harry frowned. "Stop reading?"

Rosy gasped and put a hand to Gussie's forehead. "She *must* be ill!"

Gussie moved her head away from Rosy's palm. "I meant reading so late into the night. Don't be ridiculous, the both of you. I am only fatigued."

Harry led her and Rosy through to the breakfast room where a door opened to the terrace above the garden, with its neat paths leading in and out of well-manicured hedges. Gussie took her arm off Harry's and stepped down the large shallow stairs and walked down the path at a brisk pace.

"That's better," she said, hoping they would believe her. But ten steps into her march her exhausted body protested so much that she was forced to slow her steps. She put a hand to her head and blew out a deep breath.

"Gussie!"

Behind her, Harry's boots crunched against the pebbles on the path, and an instant later she was surrounded by one of his arms and crushed against his side. "You're not going to faint, are you?" he asked.

When had he become so strong? She was not faint but felt sure that if her knees happened to buckle while she was still in Harry's embrace, gravity would have no effect on her. He wouldn't let it.

"Harry, I am well, really," she said and tried to extricate herself from his hold on her.

"Don't lie to us. Anyone can see that you are not." He sounded almost angry.

Rosy, on the other side of her, pointed to the middle of the garden. "Bring her over to the fountain so she can sit down. And don't make her walk, Harry."

And how would he do that, pray? Gussie turned wide eyes to his face. "Harry, if you dare—"

In one sweeping motion Harry lifted her and scooped up her legs in his other arm. "Will you be quiet and let us help you? You are as stubborn as a mule. There's no bearing with you sometimes."

"Then put me down and leave me alone."

"No."

"Gussie, what is the matter with you?" Rosy asked as if she couldn't believe her ears.

If Gussie had marveled about Harry's strength a moment before, she was in complete awe of how easily he carried her now. She was not large or tall, but she knew how one's mass and the pull of gravity worked on this planet. Harry made her feel as if she weighed no more than a feather.

They came up to the stone fountain, dry now for the winter months. Harry deposited her on the edge and sat so close to her that their knees touched. He bent such a frown at her that her next snappish retort dried on her tongue. "I am about to fetch the doctor for you, you're behaving that disturbingly. Do I need to do that? You need to talk to us, Gus."

The threat of medical intervention was as good as a box across the ears. Gussie sat stock still, looking from Harry to Rosy. Rosy really did look frightened.

Shame for her behavior crept into Gussie's heart. True, she had never before had to face such feelings as she felt now, but that was no excuse for behaving like a child and worrying her friends. But Harry's demand to talk to them? To tell them what was going on, to tell *Harry* what was wrong? No.

She took a steadying breath and folded her hands together on her lap. She tried relaxing her shoulders, but it was hard on such a chill, overcast day. She had gone straight outside with no thought of a pelisse or bonnet. "There is no need for the doctor. Forgive me. I will be well shortly."

Harry's expression did not soften much at her assurance. He lifted his hand and placed it on hers. "Are you certain? Your hands are chilled. We shouldn't stay out here long."

Rosy nodded, agreeing with Harry, but her eyes never left their hands. It was as if she was in a trance. Gussie tried to make herself move her hands out from under Harry's, but their warmth was too comforting to leave just yet.

With a little jerk of her head, Rosy seemed to come back into the present. "Let me get you a glass of wine, Gussie. Perhaps that will help. Harry, you stay out here with her. I won't be a moment."

***

Rosy ran off like a shot back to the house before either Harry or Gussie beside him could protest. They stayed where they were, but Harry felt Gussie slide her hands out from under his. The cool air that took up the space sent an unpleasant chill creeping across his skin.

They sat silent, neither looking the other in the face. Rosy had better hurry with that wine. He wouldn't keep Gussie out here much longer. But they were alone, truly alone for the first time since he'd come back. Since he had fallen in love with her. Gussie may not like surprises, but if he never told her how he felt, if he never took the chance that she might, *might* say yes after all, he would spend the rest of his life married to someone else but still be wondering what Gussie might have said.

Without meeting her eye, he leaned his head toward her. "Just to confirm that we understand one another, that night at the Welbeck's, before we went into dinner...I told you that we were silly, stupid children. Remember?"

He looked up right as Gussie snapped her head forward as if trying not to get caught looking at him. "Yes," she said tightly.

"I was referring to that promise we made to each other, you know, with that dull knife of mine—" He lifted his hand, displaying the scar.

"I remember. What of it?"

He could almost feel the air surrounding her becoming agitated, though there was no breeze. He hastened to reassure her. "I meant what I said, we shouldn't give such a foolish thing another thought. How could we know what things would come to pass? I don't hold you to it."

"Nor I you."

"Exactly, but Gussie..." He paused only a moment before taking the plunge. "What if I find that I want to be near you more and more? What if I were to ask if you might allow me to be more than just your old friend?"

Gussie sat so still he wondered if she was still breathing. The only indication she had not turned to stone was her eyes darting here and there without focusing on anything.

"What are you saying?" she finally asked.

"You've had the conviction never to marry for I don't know how long, but," he bent his head and looked down at his clasped hands. "Would it really be so bad, being married to me?"

A little gasp escaped her as she turned away from him, but she remained sitting.

"I know you hold marriage in disdain. You're incredibly independent and too intelligent for your own good sometimes. But if you're afraid that I'd rule over you and stop you from doing the things you love, I promise you I wouldn't."

A chuckle escaped him as an image entered his head of him standing, a high and mighty husband, over a bowed and docile little Gussie, telling her she could not read the books in the library that day. Little wife would be disappointed, but would bend her head low, meekly accepting her husband's order. It was more than laughable. "You wouldn't let me."

Gussie still had not moved, but a sniff from her had him hunting for his handkerchief in his pocket. Perfect. He had made her cry, and he had a feeling those weren't tears of joy from a damsel receiving a most wanted proposal.

He reached over and pressed his hand against her shoulder, twitching the handkerchief with his fingers to bring her attention to it. She looked down just enough to see why and accepted the handkerchief without a word.

Harry let the white cloth slip through his fingers as she pulled it away, but he did not pull back his hand. Rather, he turned his palm over and rested it on her shoulder. "Gus, please say something. Would you give me a chance?"

Silence stretched between them. It only lasted a few seconds, but it might as well have been an eternity for him. What she would say would either send him into the clouds with ecstasy at being given the mere chance to court her or crush his spirits entirely.

"Harry," she said at last, "I am so afraid."

Afraid? Of him? Harry inched closer to her. "I don't understand. Afraid of what? Gussie, it's *me*. You've never been afraid of me. Quite the opposite, really, believe me."

"It's not that," she said, finally shifting her position to better face him. "It is only—I can't have children, Harry. I simply can't."

She ended this surprising confession by applying the handkerchief to her nose as she held back the tears that were gathering in her eyes.

Harry's eyes narrowed as he tried to make sense of what she had just said. "Can't have—but how do you know? Did a doctor tell you, or—"

"No. It's not that. I am not barren. That is, I shouldn't think I am, I don't know. It's not that I know I *can't* have children, it's that I don't—*want* to."

Yes, that would put a damper of things, having a wife who didn't want children. "But that is easily fixed with nurses and governesses and tutors. I wouldn't ask you to raise them and be forever tied to them," he said.

"No, Harry, you don't understand." Gussie took her lips between her teeth, obviously distressed. Harry wanted nothing more than to take her in her arms and make all her worries go away. But he held back and waited for her to finish, which she did haltingly. "I am not afraid of children once they are here, but of the process of *getting* them here."

"Getting them here?" Harry asked. This impromptu proposal was running away with him. "You mean...what do you mean?"

She gave him a hard look. "The ordeal. What a woman has to go through to bring a child into the world. You cannot promise I would not die in childbirth. All the nurses and governess and tutors in the world could not stop that from happening. And I don't want to die."

"You wouldn't die, Gussie—"

"But you can't promise that I would make it through the ordeal, can you? Only God knows."

As much as he wanted to, he couldn't argue that. He reached his hand over to try to possess hers once more to comfort her. The instant he moved she shot up from their stone seat faster than a bullet and began pacing in front of him. Harry was so confused that he remained sitting, studying her intently.

"But even before that. What a husband and wife must do in order to—to—" She gesticulated wildly with her hands and ended up placing them on the top of her head. She turned away from him, sniffing loudly.

Harry mouthed her last few words as his mind raced to keep up with hers. "Must do in order to—ah," he said slowly as it struck him.

He stood and stepped up to her. Her back was turned to him and though the desire to wrap his arms around her, pressing her into him to provide a warm, solid barrier against her fears, was so overpowering, he held the urge back. "Now where did you learn about that, I wonder?" he asked, then almost laughed. "What am I saying? You're Gussie Stilwell. Why wouldn't you know about that? You know just about everything else, though I find it hard to believe your father's library had a volume on it."

He needed to stop talking. He was becoming much too familiar, too intimate. Gussie may be his best friend, but she was still a lady, the daughter of a baronet. He couldn't treat her like one of his fellow soldiers. If he didn't get his nervousness under control, his tongue would wag him to ruin.

"Servants talk, when they're paid enough," she replied. "Though that was a time when I wish I had not been so curious. I could have done without *that* knowledge. If anything, it only furthered my resolve never to marry." She turned her head slightly toward him. "Have I shocked you, knowing about such things? Society would certainly put me down as a vulgar lost cause if they knew I know."

Harry tossed the idea around in his head. "I don't think you're the only unmarried woman in the ton to know about it, but yes, it would probably keep you out of Almack's."

"I've never been. I offended Lady Castlereagh in my first season. I can't even remember what I said, but I was never given a voucher."

Harry chuckled softly. "That's right, you told me. I'd forgotten."

Though he laughed at the memory, he was finally beginning to realize that the qualms that Gussie had over marriage were not solely based on pride and a desire for independence. Her fears were real and deep, if the anxious light in her eye told him anything. Her chafing against the possibility of a husband ruling in tyranny over her was something he was sure he could coax her away from, given their history. If anything, he would be in danger of being ruled over by her. As for her apprehensions over the marital relations in which a husband and wife engaged, he felt sure he could win her over on that head too, given enough time. If they married, he might become a husband, but he was her friend first and had been for years. Her comfort would be paramount. Perhaps her informant had presented the information in a bad or frightening light.

But a fear of dying? How could he calm that fear when he had no say in what God willed or not? He knew full well how powerless a person could be when it came to death. One never knew the time or place, no matter what one did. His brother, John, was proof of that. So was his cousin George.

But could one not hope? Did hope have nothing to say? "Gussie, will you turn around and look at me for one minute?"

Fidgeting, she slowly turned, but her eyes didn't rise above his chest. He took a step toward her, praying she wouldn't step back and keep the distance between them. Her shoulders stiffened, but she stayed where she was. "You might not die, you know. Many mothers don't," he said softly.

"But some do," she whispered back.

"I know. And you're right. I couldn't promise that it wouldn't happen. I know that as well as anyone. But Gussie, I love you so, so dearly. Putting that aside, is there anything else in me that would make you recoil from becoming my wife? You're fond of me, but could you not think of me as a friend *and* a husband? Could you not love me too?"

Gussie closed her eyes hard, her lips trembling. He was not sorry for what he said, but to see her in such distress wrung his heart. He closed the space between them and grasped her arms in a gentle hold, as if he thought he might keep her frame from breaking into pieces. A small sob escaping her nearly undid him, and he moved to bring her into him, but she lifted her hands in front of her, placed them on his chest and pushed away from him.

Harry then watched as she made a supreme effort to control herself. A deep breath, shoulders straightening, closed eyes, and she was back to the calm, composed Augusta Stilwell. "It is not possible, Harry," she said.

Harry's jaw tightened. "I don't believe that."

"It is when you have promised to marry before the year is out. That is only two weeks away."

"Engaged before the year is out," Harry corrected.

"But married as quickly as possible," Gussie returned. "Is that not so? That is what you promised your mother?"

Harry bowed his head. "Yes, but—"

"That is that, then. You are master of Camrose now, Harry, and you need to marry. You *should* marry. And you should marry someone who will do her duty and not be as stubborn or as contrary as I am. Really, Harry, I am doing you a favor. You may not realize it now, but—only don't marry Amelia Blackwell. I couldn't stand it if you—"

"I am not marrying Amelia Blackwell," Harry said with a bite in his voice. This was getting out of hand. "I don't want someone who will *do their duty* by me. I want you."

He saw Gussie's face begin to crumple before she turned away again. "It wouldn't be fair to you," she said.

"And just what does *that* mean?" Harry asked. But before he could press the matter, a movement from the house caught his eye. He didn't know how long she had been there, but his mother had just moved away from a window. How long had she been watching them?

"I must go now," Gussie said over her shoulder. "I don't want to talk about this anymore. And I am freezing."

Now Harry felt like a brute. A crushed, broken-hearted brute. Here he was in a waistcoat and jacket when she wore no more than a thin muslin day dress. But when he moved to take off his jacket and offer it to her, she stopped him. "Please, I am well enough. Just allow me to go back into the house. I need to recover myself; they can't see me like this. Leave me alone, please."

She paused, giving Harry enough space to pray she would say something, anything, to give him a tiny ray of hope.

"I am sorry, Harry," she whispered and walked back to the house.

Chapter Fifteen

Alone in her room sometime later, Gussie leaned her head against both her hands and released a great sigh. She had excused herself from accompanying the Barrett family to dinner at the old vicar's house, pleading a headache. She felt so tired yet knew sleep would never reach her if she were to lie down. Her mind would hold repose hostage until she sorted out these feelings that seemed set on overwhelming her.

She had almost said yes. She had almost thrown caution to the wind and flung herself into Harry's arms so he could hold her tight against her fears. She could no longer deny that part of her longed to be with Harry and to never part with him. Part of her wondered what it would feel like if he took her in his arms or rested his cheek against hers. Not only wondered but yearned for it. But whenever she gave those thoughts more than a moment's rumination, the old fears raised their ugly heads.

She did not want to marry. Why allow a man to control and possess everything she had and the inheritance she would come into when she could do it perfectly well and always to her liking? She did not want to bear children. Just the thought of going through the travail sent Gussie's heart racing with fear. So why did she want Harry so close to her, why wish he would touch her so softly? She could not fathom allowing any other man to take such a liberty. But she was beginning to fathom it with Harry.

When had this begun? The obvious answer might be when she knew the terms of the Pact had been nullified, but that answer alone did not satisfy her. Had she grown fond of him before that and been unaware of it? That didn't make sense either. She certainly hadn't loved him when he'd left for the army, nor had she felt any sort of *tendre* for him when they were children. Rosy had fallen in love with him for a month or two at one point, but that had been quickly remedied when that Harrington boy had tipped his hat and smiled at her as he rode past her cart and pony one afternoon. She had not thought of Harry since, Gussie was sure, but that was neither here nor there.

I love you so, so dearly…

Shivers went through Gussie's whole frame as she remembered Harry's words. It was obvious now that he thought he felt something toward her, but what if that was only because he had his sights set on marriage anyway?

Gussie rose from her chair and paced around the room, chewing on a fingernail as she thought. If there *was* an exact moment she had started to like Harry more than just liking him (*like him more than just liking him?* Only look how muddled her thoughts were!), she needed to find out. But where to start?

She had cultivated an off-and-on habit of keeping a diary when she was younger, but most of her entries were her thoughts on what she had been studying at the time. Nothing about Harry in those writings. Besides, the diaries were in London. She looked around her room at the piles of books that rested on any flat space she could find then gave a snort of laughter. No mention of Harry Fletcher in Locke's or Descartes's writings . If she wanted to really examine her feelings for Harry…

It had to be her letters to him, which was impossible. There was no way she could go to him and ask for them back.

But *his* letters to *her* might give her something.

She walked with purposeful steps to the bellpull and tugged it. She wanted those letters now but would have to wait. They were in the London house, tucked safely away in place only she knew. She would have to give very specific instructions to her maid.

While she waited for Alice to answer her summons, she continued her pacing about the room and fell to studying the paintings on the walls that she had never given much heed to. There were a few sketches of Rutland landscapes in crayon and watercolor. A painting in oil portrayed a man (likely one of Mr. Barrett's predecessors) with a gun on his shoulder and a dog at his side. The last one was of a mother with one child in her arms surrounded by three more.

Gussie stilled and studied their faces. The mother looked happy enough, the children angelic enough. Did the mother look like that all the time, or had the artist taken liberties? Perhaps he was ordered to cover up the strain in her eye when her baby started squalling, which it undoubtedly had. It was a baby after all. Gussie's little half-brother certainly had a pair of lusty lungs, and he was only a few weeks old. Could she ever look as happy as that mother did in the painting with her children gathered around her? *Harry's* children gathered around her?

Alice opened the door and stepped into the room. "Yes, miss?"

"Oh, you're here already," Gussie cried. "I meant to have your instructions ready for you. Stay where you are. It will not take long." She went to her little toiletry table (only a small corner of it actually filled with toiletries) and placed a piece of paper before her. "You are going to London."

Alice blinked her wide set eyes. "London, miss?"

"Yes," Gussie said as she dipped the pen in the little silver ink standish. "I need something from the house. It is very important. You will leave first thing in the morning on the stage in Ryhall, spend the night in town, and come back the next day. While I am writing, get my outdoor things ready. I am going to visit my sister."

***

Mary did not ride.

This would have been a cardinal sin in the house of Sir Gerald Stilwell, baronet, if she did not drive so beautifully as she did now with Gussie sitting next to her. Her talent with the ribbons had become apparent at a young age, and now, at nearly seventeen, she was credited as one of the finest young drivers if not in London, certainly in their neighborhood of Rutland. Each of them had a rug draped over their laps and wrapped around their feet, for though the sun shined bright, the December afternoon was chill.

When Gussie had arrived at her father's house to ask Mary to take her for a drive in her own little phaeton, Mary had readily agreed. Since then, Gussie had hardly spoken a word. She didn't exactly wish to talk about her troubles to anyone, but she wanted company. Company that she didn't have to check herself, with whom she could speak her mind openly with complete trust in their discretion.

Her little sister Mary was the first person to come to mind.

Mary, used to her ways, did not press her but rather told her of the happenings among the guests in their father's house. The still life that she and her friends had painted that morning. How everyone had laughed when one of Sir Gerald's spaniels had tripped on the turf while running after a stick and slid for what seemed ages on the wet grass. Once Mary ran out of things to say, silence settled between them. Not an awkward silence, but one of contented companionship for which Gussie was grateful.

It wasn't until Mary turned her pair of bays back toward Oakleigh, some five miles away by now, that Gussie began to speak. "What would you do if you did not wish to marry, but a little piece of you did?" she asked, fiddling her fingers inside her muff.

It was more than a little piece, but just admitting it out loud was a feat.

Mary gave the question some thought before answering. "I'm not entirely sure. I don't have a little piece of me wanting to marry. Every piece of me wants to marry."

Gussie smiled at her sister and leaned into her plump figure affectionately. "And I hope you do. I know you will. You'll make the biggest splash in London when you come out and make a brilliant match before the Season is half over."

Mary gave her a look that questioned her intelligence. "I am not pretty enough for that. But tell me what you are thinking. What, or who, has you changing your mind?"

So, Gussie told her all that had happened, beginning with the making of the Pact up to when Harry had all but asked her to marry him that morning. Mary listened earnestly to all Gussie had to say and was silent for some time at the end of the tale. "Do you know, I am not surprised," she said at last. "He is fearfully handsome."

"It is not that he is handsome. Well, one cannot deny that he *is* handsome. But that is not why I am having doubts."

"Have you fallen in love with him?"

Gussie grimaced. "No. Perhaps? No!" She brought her hands up to her cheeks, pink from the cold. "I don't know. Truly. I promised myself I would never marry, you know that."

Mary nodded. "But then you promised to marry Harry if he inherited Camrose."

"Which was supposed to be impossible!"

Mary shook her head in wonder. "You are right. It is the strangest thing."

"The most barbaric thing, you mean. I made the stipulation back then that two people would have to die (no, *three* people, for his cousin's father was still alive back then), before I would marry him, and look what has happened. And I was only ten!"

"But you didn't wish for their deaths. You didn't want to marry, even back then. It is not your fault that they all died."

To Gussie's surprise, hot tears stung the backs of her eyes. She quickly blinked them away. "It doesn't feel right somehow. And he said he must be engaged by the new year. It is so fast. Much too fast."

"Then don't marry him."

"But I...oh!" Gussie cried out in frustration. "I don't know what I want anymore."

Mary took the lines in one hand and wrapped an arm around Gussie, squeezing her once. "I wish Diana were here. She would know what to tell you better than I. Phyllis would say it was your duty to accept him if Harry made you an offer. Papa would wish it too, I imagine. For myself, I can't say that I understand what you are going through. I've always wanted to marry. I've never wished to be independent or to manage my own money or affairs. Except for my secret...well, you know. And even with your help, that has been the most confusing thing! And I wish to be a mother. Say what you like about little Gerald and his screaming, our brother is a darling, and I cannot wait to have children of my own."

Gussie sighed. Mary might change her mind about children if she knew what had to happen in order to become with child.

"But I am glad you told me all this. I only wish I could help you more," Mary continued.

"You have done, dearest. I may not know what to do, but I feel lighter now that I've said these things out loud. I'll find my way. Don't worry."

"I know you will. You are so much cleverer than Diana or me. It is only, I don't think you should pass up this opportunity lightly just to keep up the convictions you've had for so long. Harry may have to marry quickly, but you have known him forever. It takes you so long to trust someone enough to let them see how much you can love. If Harry has become one of those happy few, I think it might make you happy as well if you tried it."

"Mary, marriage is not something you try. It isn't a book that you can pick up and put down again if you do not care for it. I couldn't treat Harry that way unless I was sure."

"You're right. I didn't mean to sound so flippant. I would just be so happy for you if you found that you wanted to marry after all."

"That makes one of us, for now anyway," Gussie replied. Until Harry's letters were brought to her, she could do no more than fret over the conundrum with her best friend. "I don't want to go back to Broadstone. It's too close to him, and I need to think."

"Papa expects you for Christmas and that is only a few days away. You could stay here."

Gussie pressed her lips together. "I do not wish to give offense to Mr. and Mrs. Barrett. They'll wonder why I left so suddenly."

Mary thought for a moment. "They will understand because I asked you to come early."

"But you haven't asked me."

"I am asking you now," Mary replied with a smirk.

Chapter Sixteen

May 1811

> *...I am at home in our London house tonight while Diana and
> our aunt are at Almack's without me, for I have not obtained
> a voucher. Who would have thought that when Lady Castle-
> leagh asked our opinion on her bonnet from a new milliner, she
> was not looking for the truth? The scold Diana and my aunt
> gave me!...*

Since he did not receive any word saying otherwise, Harry rode to the regular spot where he met Gussie and Rosy for their morning ride as planned. He rubbed a hand over his face as he posted down the road. It had been a restless night for him. He was not one to dwell much on the past. What was done was done, and since there was no changing it, the best action was to move forward.

But not this time.

He'd tossed and turned the whole night through while he played and replayed his conversation with Gussie in his head. He always came up with the same conclusion: there wasn't anything he could have said or done to make her change her mind.

The fears he longed to put to rest for her were beyond his control, and to give such a promise would be nothing short of capricious. He could not control whether a woman lived or died in childbirth. They could take all the precautions. He could have all the best doctors in England to attend to her, and still she could, *could* die. Harry held no such fears that she would, but he didn't know how to calm hers.

He had ridden out late, so he wasn't surprised that two figures on horseback were already at the meeting place waiting for him. What sent his heart plummeting to his feet was that only one of the figures was that of a lady. Rosy. The other rider was a groom.

Rosy lifted her whip in greeting as he came up to her. "You only have to put up with me today," she said. "Gussie is at Oakleigh until after Christmas. Mary wanted her."

Mary wanted her? Yes, Harry would lay a monkey that was the reason she had left. He tried not to show on his face just how hurt he was at this. It wasn't Rosy's fault, but bitter disappointment was quickly flooding over his usual carefree disposition. He gave a thoughtful noise, aware of the groom standing well within earshot. Rosy was also staring at him rather keenly. "That's a shame. It is quite a dismal day, isn't it? Come on, then. I don't want any rain catching us again."

Rosy fell in with him while giving her groom direction to ride well behind. "Since it is only me, Mama insisted that I take him with me. I think she still has hopes of making a lady out of me one of these days."

"You, a lady? When hell freezes—forgive me. I forgot who I was with." Harry gave himself an internal smack upside the head. He needed to check his feelings. That was no way to speak to Rosy.

True to form, Rosy's laugh came out clear and strong. She was always so good at seeing a joke in everything, bless her. "You are not wrong. Poor Mama. She has six sons and nearly all of them have done her and Papa proud. Two lawyers, two navy men, a clerk, and a parson with ten grandchildren between them so far. Why can't they give just one of us up for loss, and why can't it be me?"

"You may be a lost cause, but that doesn't mean I am going to start cursing in front of you," Harry retorted.

Rosy grinned. "You're put out. What's wrong?"

Harry gritted his teeth. Plenty was wrong. "Business."

"Estate business or Gussie Stilwell business?"

Harry bent a dangerous stare at her. She had run away to fetch Gussie a glass of wine, leaving them alone, and had only reappeared when the Broadstone party was about to leave. Her excuse had been that Mrs. Barrett had needed her, but now Harry was sure that hadn't been true.

Rosy didn't seem to realize the danger she was in. "Did you talk about anything interesting yesterday while I was gone?"

"Rosy."

The tone of his voice had the desired effect. Rosy's mischievous expression went slack, her eyes full of surprise. "Oh. I'm sorry. I thought...I thought you would have liked to have a moment alone together."

"And why is that?" Harry growled.

"If you are going to make me say it...you are, aren't you? Because you're in love with her, that's why."

Oh, the devil.

"I am, am I?" Harry retorted. "And how do you think you know that?"

"The way you look at her. Really, Harry, it's like you think you are the only two people in the room when you look at her. Did you really think I wouldn't notice my two friends falling in love with each other?"

Harry snapped his head toward her. "With each other? What do you mean? Gussie's not in love with me."

"I think she is, she just doesn't know it. I've thought for weeks now that the two of you should get married."

A frown settled deeper onto Harry's brow. She wouldn't be saying all this if she knew what has passed between him and Gussie the day before. "You don't know what you're talking about."

Rosy huffed. "Perhaps I don't, but I think I do. I also think you should go to Oakleigh and see her. Mary may have needed her, but it was perfectly clear to anyone watching that she was agitated and wanted to go. I know something has happened, and you need to fix it. You need to see her again."

And do what, exactly? Press Gussie further to marry him? That would only push her away. Pretend that nothing happened between them? Delusional. Apologize for loving her?

Never.

He didn't know what to do, and the topic was smarting too much to allow Rosy to continue. "That's enough, Rosy."

"But—"

"I mean it!"

Startled and wide-eyed only for a moment at the vehemence in his voice, Rosy shrugged and urged her horse into a canter. "Just a suggestion."

The remainder of their ride was stiff and constrained. They turned back for home sooner than usual. Once back at Camrose, Harry locked himself up in his study until breakfast. With Amy and Charlotte eating and chattering away with their mother, Harry took the meal mostly in silence but saw Mrs. Fletcher watching him more than once.

She had not had a chance to ask him about what she had seen through the window. As soon as Gussie had left with Rosy and Mrs. Barrett, Harry had ordered his horse to be brought up and posted over the countryside for a long while before stopping for something to eat at an alehouse. When he came home, he had shut himself up in his study to go over accounts and estate business, not to be disturbed. All that time alone with his thoughts and he still had not come up with a way to fix things with Gussie.

The butler appeared in front of him bearing a silver tray, shifting him away from his dismal, unfocused woolgathering. He took up the pile of letters from the post and began sorting them. One was addressed to him in a hand he did not recognize. Breaking away the wafer, Harry opened the mystery note. The message was short, but Harry grinned and laughed at its contents. "Splendid!"

"What is it?" Amy asked.

He looked up. All eyes were on him, waiting. "Mama," he said. "Have the best guest chambers prepared. We are having company for Christmas."

***

It had taken Alice an extra day to come back from London with Harry's letters. If Gussie wasn't mad enough for Bedlam before those unexpected twenty-four hours, she certainly was after.

"I'm sorry, miss. I couldn't find them the first night, so I missed the stage," Alice said late in the evening two days before Christmas.

It took every ounce of control Gussie had not to rip the bundle of letters from her maid's hand, but to allow Alice to place them on her open palm. Six letters. Six letters had continued their friendship over the course of four years. Harry had nine from her. "You are here now. Thank you, Alice."

Gussie would have devoured them that very minute, but there was still dinner and an evening of entertaining guests with Mary and their older cousin, Elizabeth, whom Sir Gerald had asked to play hostess since Diana and Phyllis were in London.

If ever an evening dragged on, this one did. Gussie did her duty by her father's guests to the best of her ability, but her best was quite dismal at the moment. "Why do you look at the clock so much?" Mary asked at one point. Gussie applied herself better to the task at hand after that, but while she played her part on the outside, inside she was as eager to fly away as a horse who had taken the bit in its teeth.

As soon as she could manage it without appearing rude, she excused herself for the night and tripped up to her room as fast as she could. She tapped her foot and played with the fabric of first her dress, then her nightgown while Alice helped her undress. The last time she had done that, Harry's hand had taken the place of the fabric. It hadn't been flimsy or as smooth as a silk dress, but warm, solid, and rough. It felt, oh, what was the word she was looking for?

Whole and safe.

Like home.

Sending Alice away, Gussie reached under her pillow where she had put the letters for safekeeping. Her fingers closed around them, tied together by an orange ribbon. She'd chosen that color when Harry, waxing poetic in a rare moment in one of his first letters, had described an Indian sunset. She had a feeling the ribbon's hue did not do the spectacle justice.

She crawled into her bed, hardly taking time to situate the pillows to her liking before sliding the top letter out from under the ribbon. The first letter he'd written after she had sent him a letter via Gus Stillman. The paper was cheap but still crisp. She had only read his letters two, maybe three times over when they'd arrived.

She unfolded it and was met with Harry's careless scrawl: *Gus Stillman, you minx. What do you think you're doing? I laughed so hard when your letter came that I had to come up with a lie that would stave off the curiosity of my fellow soldiers. They wanted to know what the joke was. I'm fond enough of you to take care that none of them ever find out that a baronet's daughter is writing to a lowly soldier, though after this prank, it's no more than you deserve if they do disparage you...*

A smile crept up Gussie's mouth. It was instantly followed by a scowl. He was 'fond enough' of her to take care of her reputation, but that didn't mean he had loved her then. He was looking out for her because he knew what a lady should and should not do. She, too, knew very well the rules society imposed on the daughter of a baronet. One wrong move and a lady's reputation was gone forever.

She rolled her eyes over the thought. It was completely ridiculous, the dictates of society a lady was bound to! But no one around her seemed to think the same as she did, or even acknowledge that there was much of a problem with the current system. But that was neither here nor there. She glanced over at her candle. Good. A new one, replaced that very morning. She settled into the pillows and found her place again in the letter. This was going to be a long night.

***

Gussie didn't know exactly what time it was. The little clock on the mantelpiece above the fireplace was too far away to see in the dark, though the length of her candle told her she had been studying Harry's letters for several hours.

And she had come up with nothing. His writing had never been eloquent or detailed. There had been many a time where she could have pulled her hair in frustration at the lack of description he gave when answering the questions she'd written to him, but there was no indication of anything romantic in any of the six letters. They were the letters of one friend to another, nothing more. For all she could gather from them, he had not loved her while he was in India. So why had he said he loved her so dearly? When did the shift happen?

She could probably ask him these intimate questions now, since he had proposed. She would have a right to investigate further into the matter of marriage and the feelings surrounding it if only she had not rebuffed him so. And as she sat there in the light of a single candle trying desperately to delve into Harry's mind, another hindrance arose.

Reading his letters, letters that had no declarations of love, no poetry or pretty language meant to catch and keep her heart, Gussie admitted fully and completely now that she could not do without him in her life.

She, too, loved him so, so dearly.

Chapter Seventeen

Mrs. Fenton and her three children were as good and delightful as Harry remembered them when they had boarded the ship in Lisbon, bound for England to join her husband who had been sent ahead of them on assignment.

Captain Fenton was a serious-minded man with a strict sense of duty, but perfectly amiable within that realm. He had written to Harry from an inn in a town not far from Ryhall, saying he wished to visit Camrose to express his appreciation for Harry's attentiveness to his wife and children during their journey. There was no mention of Harry's invitation to Christmas, and while Harry liked the man better for it, he immediately posted to the White Hart and made it plain to them in no uncertain terms that he wished them to be guests at Camrose for the holiday and soon had them installed comfortably in his house.

The Fenton children, aged twelve, nine, and five, were immediately picked up by Amy and Charlotte, who went to great measures to entertain them and instill the spirit of the upcoming holiday in them while the adults gathered in the drawing room for refreshments. The fresh atmosphere of new people in the house did Harry some good but didn't completely take his mind off his present predicament. Gussie was still ever-present in his thoughts.

Mrs. Fenton, a plain but pleasing woman of about four and thirty, began going on about Harry's kindness to her on the ship, which made Mrs. Fletcher glow with pride. "Not a day went by that Sir Harry did not play some game with the children to help pass the time," said Mrs. Fenton. "Even in the foul weather when we were all cooped up down below, he could joke them out of their complaints and tears, which made it a great deal easier on me, I will tell you."

She rested a hand on the swell of her belly and cast a knowing look at Mrs. Fletcher, who nodded understandingly. Harry would never have guessed she had been with child on the ship. He had put it down to seasickness.

Once refreshments had been enjoyed, Mrs. Fenton begged to excuse herself to rest in her room. Captain Fenton escorted her, leaving Harry and Mrs. Fletcher to themselves in the drawing room. Before Harry could excuse himself, his mother looked him in the eye. "Might I have a word?"

Harry knew what she wished to talk about. No part of him was looking forward to seeing her reaction to what he had to say. But now was as good a time as any. It had to be done. He leaned against the mantlepiece and nodded.

"The ball is only a week away," Mrs. Fletcher said, gently. "I hesitate to press the matter. I told you what I would like in a daughter-in-law but that I would not interfere with your choice. Would you tell me what you are thinking, though?"

The look in his mother's eye told him what she was really asking: *what happened between you and Gussie in the garden?*

Harry brought his hand up and rested his forehead against it. Time to disappoint his mother. "I asked Gussie to marry me."

Mrs. Fletcher pressed her lips together and nodded slowly. "And why have you not asked me to wish you joy until now? You might have told me right away."

"Because you made it very plain that you didn't wish her for my bride. Besides, she said no."

Mrs. Fetcher froze, her eyes wide. "What do you mean she said no? She rejected you? Why I—"

She tried to speak again, but the anger Harry could see building up prevented her. "Why are you put out by it?" he asked. "I thought you would be relieved."

"And so I am, but really, since you *did* propose, I am at a loss as to why she would not accept you. She is a most unnatural girl!"

He stared hard at his mother for a long moment. "Mama, you cannot have it both ways. First, you don't wish me to choose Gussie, but then when I do, you are offended that she rejected me. Which one do you really want?"

Mrs. Fletcher waved a hand at him while the other sought for her handkerchief. "Don't get cross, my darling. I hardly understand it myself." Having found it, she pressed the handkerchief to her nose while she controlled her emotions. "You are the only son I have left. You mean the world to me, and I would give you the moon if I could, if that was what you wanted. You deserve everything you want, and if you chose her and she rejected you...it is more than my mother's heart can bear. I tell you, I quite hate the foolish girl!"

Heated defense rushed into him at this. Her remark was as unfair as it was passionate, but he checked himself. Berating his mother would not solve anything when she was in this state. When she still felt John's loss so keenly.

He came over and knelt in front of her, taking her hands in his as she softly wept. "Dearest heart, that is a foolish thing to say. I know you. You cannot hate anyone. Not truly. Gussie's reasons for saying no are sound. I may not like them, but I cannot argue them."

"But why? Why did she then?" Mrs. Fletcher asked.

Harry shook his head. "One of the reasons is that she could not bring herself to marry so quickly as I promised you I would." That was the least important reason, but that was all he would give her. He loved his mother, but he would not relate the whole of his rejected proposal to her. It smarted too much.

"Well, to be sure," said Mrs. Fletcher. "If she had no thought of marriage before, it would come as a shock."

Harry could see that she still was not pleased at all with the situation, but nothing he could say or do could alleviate her distress. Time would soothe her ruffled feathers. "I must go. I promised the girls I would take them into Ryhall with the Fenton children, and I haven't even had the horses put to yet." He pressed her hands one last time. "It will work itself out, Mama. But while I will try, don't expect an engagement to be announced at the ball. I'm not going to fall over dead tomorrow, you know."

She said nothing. Only giving a small nod as she stared off into nothing, deep in thought. Harry's heart wrung for her. She and Gussie were more similar in their fears than either of them realized.

He rose and headed for the door. Just before he reached it, Mrs. Fletcher turned and said between sniffs, "Dearest, I know we agreed what should happen, but sometimes happiness takes more time than we like. I wish you to marry and quickly, but I do so wish you to be happy with your choice. I can be a little patient."

He did not turn but only nodded before walking out of the room, his heart smarting with each step. She would be waiting a long time.

***

Christmas Day in her father's house was a dismal affair for Gussie. Not because there was anything wanting in Mary and Cousin Elizabeth's preparations for the holiday. The house was decked out in all the greenery that a proper English country house should have, while guests feasted on mince pies and venison with plenty of ale and wine. It had been four days since her discovery of her real love for Harry. Six days without a sight of him. She didn't know how many more she would have to bear, for in saying no to Harry, she was sure she had lost him forever.

The very thing she was afraid of, losing his friendship, had come to pass, and it was of her own doing. How could she recover a friendship when she had hurt Harry so much? She had seen it in his eyes that day at the fountain, and now, so many days later, she couldn't hit upon any scenario that could repair the fracture between them.

At the breakfast table the day after Christmas, the morning post was presented. Letters and notes were passed around to their intended recipients. "From Diana," Mary said, eagerly showing Gussie the direction written in Diana's flowing, elegant hand. "Shall we go upstairs to read it?"

Gussie gave Mary's arm a squeeze. "You go, darling. I find that I need some air."

Mary looked at her. "Didn't you get enough on your ride this morning?"

"No. I need more." What she really longed for was some solitude, even though all her moments of seclusion over the past few days had done nothing to make her feel better.

Before Mary could respond, one of the footmen appeared on Gussie's left. "A note for you, miss. Come round from Camrose."

Gussie's heart froze for one petrifying moment as she stared down at the piece of paper in the footman's gloved hand. Just as quickly as it had stopped, her heart revived itself with a vigor that she had never felt before. It was a wonder Mary could not hear its pounding. A wave of heat rushed up her entire body but still she could not move.

Not taking her eyes off her, Mary slowly reached out her hand and took the note from the footman herself. "Thank you," she said to him and looked at the note. "It is a woman's hand. Shall I open it for you?"

A woman's hand. That meant it was not from Harry. Finally, she moved enough to take it from Mary. "I have it."

Unfolding the paper, she immediately looked at the bottom of the page. *Maria Fletcher.* What did Harry's mother want? Gussie's eyes trailed back up to the top of the letter and took in its short message. "Mrs. Fletcher is asking us to luncheon today if we are not engaged elsewhere. Are we...are we engaged elsewhere today? I cannot remember."

Mary shook her head. "Nothing of consequence. Let's go. Do say you'll go." She lowered her voice so the others at the table would not hear her. "Harry may be there, and he may not. But you've been miserable for days. Couldn't you talk to Harry and still be friends?"

That mountain seemed impossible to climb, but the desire to see him again was so poignant, and here was an opportunity to do just that, given by his own mother. "I suppose we could go over," Gussie said.

"We will," Mary replied with a brightness that Gussie found exhausting in her present state of mind. How little beams of sunshine could bounce off her sister at a time like this was baffling. Mary was probably hoping that she and Harry would come to an understanding and get married after all. Though she was not even seventeen, the sooner Mary was married herself, the better.

At the appointed time, they came to Camrose in Mary's phaeton. Gussie's insides were dancing some sort of barbaric, pounding reel within her as they were escorted not to Mrs. Fletcher's preferred saloon in the back of the house, but to the drawing room. Once the butler had announced them, Gussie took a deep, steadying breath and walked in.

One subtle glance about the room told her Harry was not there. She didn't know whether to breathe a sigh of relief or start crying. But it was not just the Fletcher women in the drawing room.

Another woman and a girl of no more than twelve or thirteen, perhaps, were with them. Strangers whom Gussie had never seen before. The make of their clothes, though clean and neat, was of a plainer sort that told Gussie they did not hold as high a place in the world as the ton of England. All the ladies rose, and Gussie noted that the woman was with child.

Mrs. Fletcher came to them. "Thank you for coming. Pray, let me acquaint you with some friends of ours. Miss Stilwell, Miss Mary Stilwell, this is Mrs. Fenton and her daughter, Miss Fenton.

Fenton. Fenton. Gussie's mind darted about here and there trying to recover the name. It was an important one. Important to Harry.

Mrs. Fenton bent her head gracefully and moved to shake their hands. "How do you do?" she said in an easy, cheerful manner. "Mrs. Fletcher's daughters have told me so much about you, I already know I shall like you."

Gussie and Mary each dipped into a small curtsy to the older woman. *Fenton. Fenton.* Why couldn't Gussie think? *And do* not *stare at her middle so,* she said harshly to herself. It was a hard thing not to do. There was an infant inside Mrs. Fenton doing Gussie could not guess what, and here was Mrs. Fenton smiling calmly at them as if nothing of import was going on inside her. Oh! Fenton!

"You are the Mrs. Fenton who was on the ship with Sir Harry," Gussie said at the exact moment Mrs. Fletcher opened her mouth to speak.

Mrs. Fletcher nodded but her smile was tight. "Indeed. The very same."

"Yes, I am," Mrs. Fenton said. "I was so obliged to him during that voyage. His kindness to the children exceeded everything. Mrs. Fletcher tells me that it was all fun and games to him, but he was such a help to me that my husband wished to thank him in person."

Amy spoke up. "They have been here for Christmas. We've all had such fun, haven't we?"

"Indeed, we have," Mrs. Fletcher agreed. "Luncheon won't be ready for some minutes. Let me take you to the south lawn and introduce Captain Fenton to you. He and Harry are playing with the other children. Come."

Chapter Eighteen

Here it was. The moment Gussie would see Harry again. Her heartbeat picked up and she felt as if she might be sick, her stomach dropped so, but she followed the rest of the women outdoors.

The clacking of wooden sticks and ferocious war cries greeted her ears before she caught sight of anyone, and soon she saw Harry fighting for his life against two small boys. Each had a long stick perfect for swordplay. An older man, not so tall as Harry, with thinning hair atop his head, stood a few paces away leaning on his stick, watching.

Miss Fenton called out to him. "Why are you not playing, Papa? Are you dead?"

"Quite dead, dearest," he called back. He was about to turn back to the battle, but then noticed Gussie and Mary. He straightened up and walked over to them.

Mrs. Fletcher introduced Captain Fenton to them. He bowed to them with military exactness as they made their curtsies. He looked to be a serious man. The stick in his hand contrasted with the sternness about his mouth, but his eyes were not hard, only clear. Gussie surmised that he was of a profound nature and wondered what stories and experiences he could offer in a conversation. But these thoughts were there and gone in a minute, for Harry had finally noticed them.

Gussie hoped she presented a calm exterior, but her breath quickened as she wondered what was going to happen next. Harry only lifted his stick in salutation before returning to the fray. "Hallo, Gussie! Hallo, Mary!"

Mary chuckled, her round cheeks plumping up as she smiled and waved back. Gussie lifted her hand only through instinct. She took a silent steadying breath and thanked the Lord that Harry had not come up to them but instead greeted them from a distance. Like a friend. That gave Gussie the time she needed to compose herself. Had Harry known she would need some distance before their next encounter?

Beside her, Mary engaged Captain Fenton, inquiring about his time in Lisbon and what action he had seen. Gussie could not focus on their words. She could only stare at Harry and wonder what was going to happen. She felt as if she were looking at him on one side of a huge chasm with him on the other, never to be close to one another again. In this vision, she saw him turn away from her, grabbing the hand of some unknown female figure and walking away, never to look at her again. He felt so far away...

She did not notice that Mrs. Fenton had stepped over to her until she spoke, breaking her dramatic daydream. "Forgive me, Miss Stilwell, but are you not the friend that Sir Harry spoke of on the ship? Are you indeed, 'Gussie'?"

Gussie raised her brows, surprised. "He spoke of me?"

"Yes. He spoke of many things to while away the time and he did mention a dear old friend of his and the things you did as children. Did he really throw a fish at you?"

Gussie closed her eyes at the mention of the embarrassing, slimy event but couldn't help smiling a little. Harry would tell a story like that if he thought it would get a laugh out of someone. "He did, horrid man."

"Wretched boy," Mrs. Fenton chuckled. "That is something my little Tom would do, if his father did not keep a strict eye on him. Always looking for mischief."

"I hope he didn't entertain you with other such shameful pranks he played on me as a child."

Mrs. Fenton lifted a reassuring hand. "The children would ask for stories mostly about his brother and their friends. You had quite a gaggle of boys in the country, as I understand it. Aside from the fish, he only mentioned you with a sort of...nostalgic fondness, if you will. It was clear you were a great friend of his."

Gussie's mind studied these words with calculations and conclusions quickly following. Mrs. Fenton said no more, but the look on her face told Gussie she thought there must be an understanding of sorts between them. He must have been in love with her before he even reached England. He had carried these feelings for weeks, perhaps months before—

"Oh!"

The little cry from Mrs. Fenton startled Gussie. She looked over to see Mrs. Fenton placing a hand on her stomach.

"What is it? Are you well?" Gussie asked.

Mrs. Fenton waved her questions off with a good-natured smile. "It is nothing. It only took me by surprise, the little devil."

She threw a fond look at her round middle, which allowed Gussie to give it a brief study. Mrs. Fenton didn't seem at all perturbed by the interruption. She carried her child so unlike Phyllis, who had been bedridden from the ordeal almost as soon as it had begun and had groaned horribly anytime the infant moved within her.

"It doesn't hurt," said Mrs. Fenton.

Gussie looked up at her. "I beg your pardon?"

Mrs. Fenton smiled. "You looked so worried. It doesn't hurt when it moves."

"At all?"

Mrs. Fenton's answer was not so quick this time. "It can be uncomfortable. Especially when one is close to confinement. But that is still a long way off."

Mrs. Fenton seemed content to leave it at that, but her kind face and easy manner emboldened Gussie's curiosity. "But that will hurt. The confinement."

Mrs. Fenton gave her a measured look. Gussie hoped she wasn't trying to decide how intrusive she thought Gussie's question was, but after a moment she said, "Yes, but that is how it has always been, since Eve, you know."

Gussie gave a nod and looked off in the direction of Harry and the children were playing. Three Fenton children and three Fletcher children. Mrs. Fenton and Mrs. Fletcher had gone through the trial of childbirth so many times, and yet Gussie could not fathom how they could do it.

"And it isn't as bad as that," Mrs. Fenton said presently.

Gussie looked an inquiry. "Sorry?"

Mrs. Fenton's smile was warm and encouraging. It reminded Gussie of her own mother's smile, the little bits of it she could remember anyway. "It is not as bad as your face is now telling me you think it is. It is an ordeal, to be sure—"

"Then why—" Gussie stopped herself before she could finish the question, *why do you do it?* She was not ignorant of the part the husbands played in the matter. "I don't understand it," she said. Playing ignorant was the safest path to take. She had no wish to offend Harry's guests.

"Of course. There is no need for you to think of such things until you are married, you know. But I must say, there is nothing quite like holding your child in your arms for the first time. Being a mother is the pride of my life."

The sentiment was clear in her face as she turned her eyes back to her children, who had Harry on the run, swinging their weapons high in the air and whooping out war cries. The other onlookers laughed heartily at the scene.

Mrs. Fletcher excused herself from Mr. Fenton and Mary and walked over to Gussie and Mrs. Fenton. "Such hearty children you have, my son's advanced years do nothing for him."

"You are very kind," Mrs. Fenton replied. "I would put a stop to it in an instant, but if I may, I believe Sir Harry likes the play just as much as they do."

Mrs. Fletcher chuckled indulgently. "One thing he takes most seriously is play. If it were up to him, we would all be running around with sticks. And he is so fond of children."

"I see that clearly and am grateful for it. I was just saying to Miss Stilwell that the pride of a woman's life is found in her children. Would you not agree with that sentiment?"

Gussie's face grew warm as Mrs. Fetcher looked at her. But the distant civility that was usually in her eyes did not appear. She hoped Mrs. Fenton was bred well enough not to disclose the other things they had been talking about.

"That is as true a statement as I ever heard," Mrs. Fletcher replied.

"Despite the hardships?" Mrs. Fenton asked.

Mrs. Fletcher nodded. "Despite the hardships."

Mrs. Fletcher turned to look on the children once more, but Mrs. Fenton caught Gussie's eye and gave her stomach a few soft pats. Then with a friendly smile and nod, she excused herself and walked over to her husband. Noticing her by his side, Captain Fenton's face softened a touch, and he leaned slightly in her direction before righting himself, by way of greeting. Mrs. Fenton moved in unison with him. Gussie couldn't see her face, but she imagined a similar expression resting on it.

There seemed to be a quiet contentment hovering around the military couple. Calm, comforting, and steady. Nothing like her father's interactions with his newly acquired wife.

Gussie could tell Sir Gerald and the new Lady Stilwell had liked each other well enough in the beginning, but their interactions had quickly become tumultuous. Especially after Phyllis became with child and grew so ill. Up until her father's marriage, Gussie had rarely made a particular study of the married couples she'd come across. If she did, it was only to find evidence of why she had made the right choice in deciding to not bother with the institution at all.

But now, seeing Captain and Mrs. Fenton's small interaction, such a little moment that was gone as soon as it had come...

She looked to the lawn. Harry and the children looked to be done playing and were heading back up to their audience. She could easily imagine Harry sharing such a moment with her as the Fentons just had.

She could not help but watch Harry as his long strides brought him closer and closer to her. His own eyes caught hers and held her gaze. There might be some hesitation in them, but Gussie thought there was something else in them as well, something that burned. Not anger, at least she hoped not. But an intensity of a sort. One she wished she could investigate further. Perhaps it meant he wasn't too far out of her reach as she imagined.

The party watched as the children came running across the lawn to them. Harry brought up the rear.

"It looks as though they have finally worn him out," Mrs. Fletcher observed, then turned to Gussie. "I wanted to express my gratitude to you, Gussie, for the lessons you taught to Amy. I know you value your time with your books. It was very kind of you. Thank you."

Gussie gave her a nod. "Amy made it very easy. She will play beautifully one day."

"Yes, I think so," agreed Mrs. Fletcher. "I hope your books will not deter you from our ball."

Gussie's stomach dropped. The ball where Harry was supposed to announce his engagement. Was he still planning to do that? He had given his word to his mother. "I am looking forward to it, ma'am."

"Splendid," Mrs. Fletcher replied.

Harry had come up to the group by now and was speaking to Mrs. Fenton and Mary. Out of the corner of her eye, Gussie saw him then turn toward her and Mrs. Fletcher. "Good day, Gussie," he said.

Before she could reply, the butler appeared at Mrs. Fletcher's elbow, informing her that luncheon was ready. "Thank you, Nelson. Let us all go inside and let the fire warm us."

Everyone agreeable, they all turned toward the house, the children running to the front with Harry's sisters chasing after them. Gussie was about to follow with the rest of the adults, but Harry's hand rested on her wrist, keeping her back until everyone else was walking in front of them.

Gussie did not look at him, nor did she give any outward appearance of being prevented from walking by the barest touch from him, but internally her entire body shivered as a fire she could not tell was hot or cold engulfed her.

Harry looked at her an instant later and swept his hand in front of him. "After you."

Gussie swallowed and stepped past him, her throat uncomfortably thick and dry. "Thank you."

He didn't let her get ahead of him but fell in next to her. Their first few strides together were conducted in silence. Gussie may have kept her composure while he was out on the lawn, but now that he was close to her, she felt a barrier, solid, stiff, and unwilling to bend, rise between them.

Should she talk to him as if nothing had happened? As if he hadn't proposed and as if she hadn't finally discovered that she loved him back?

She knew what she would tell anyone else going through such turmoil. Just make a decision to either discuss the matter like rational, civilized people, or decide you won't and move on. She had always thought other females so silly for the emotional acrobatics she had seen them display when caught up by strong passions. Fits of hysteria, fainting spells, indecisiveness, overt use of smelling salts and burnt feathers. But now a small part of her was beginning to understand what those other ladies might have been going through.

"How was Christmas at Oakleigh?" he asked, breaking through her thoughts.

"Lovely," she replied.

He huffed. "Liar."

She looked up at him. "What?"

"I have never in my life heard you describe an enormous gathering of any kind, Christmas or not, as 'lovely'. *Our* Christmas was lovely. We decked everything in green, sang dozens of carols, went to church. The girls put on a *lovely* little play act with the Fenton children. All in all, a *lovely* Christmas. But enough about our holiday." He laid a discerning eye on her. "How was *your* Christmas?"

As he talked, a lightness entered into Gussie, slowly melting and bending that unyielding bulwark that she had been feeling for days. It did not disappear entirely, but Harry's efforts to tease her like he normally did helped ease her anxieties a little. Perhaps he did not despise her as she thought he would (or should) after the scene in the garden.

"It was noisy and crowded, and my father made me play I don't know how many jigs on the piano so all the guests could dance at least twice," she replied.

She did not tell him how many sleeping hours she had lost reading and rereading his letters. How many silent tears had rolled onto her pillow as she'd lain awake miserable, certain she loved him and equally certain their friendship was over.

"At least it wasn't the harp," Harry said.

"You make a very good point. I suppose I should be more grateful. I've endured worse house parties."

Silence fell between them, and all the awkwardness was quick to return. Gussie felt it, anyway, if Harry did not. How she wished she knew what he was thinking. She could not decipher the soft light in his eye. Was it a sad light or a content light? A tired light from losing so soundly to the Fentons' children? She couldn't tell.

"Your mother is looking forward to the ball," she said. It wasn't at all what she really wanted to say, but she had to say *something.*

They had entered the house by now through a back door. Gussie couldn't bear the idea of spending an hour politely nibbling on cold meats and fruit while she was going through such turmoil inwardly. She stopped and turned to Harry. "Harry, I—"

He raised his hand. "No, Gus, let me speak first. I need to tell you something."

She pressed her lips together, not sure if she wanted to hear what he had to say or not. But in the end, knowing was better than not knowing, so she nodded and waited.

Harry shifted on his feet and looked down the hall. Gussie understood the look. They couldn't linger too long, or they would be missed. "I just wanted to say, haven't we done the silliest things as adults, you and I?"

Gussie stared at him, her brow furrowing.

Didn't we do the silliest things as children?

Those were the words he had used at the Welbeck's to release her from the Pact. Now here he was using the same words to release her from any worry or blame she may carry from refusing his hand.

What had she done to deserve such a friend?

"One would be quite a nincompoop if one paid any attention to such follies," she replied, echoing her own words from that night.

Harry's responding smile was almost enough to break her heart. "Right then, dear friend."

He took each of her gloved hands in his and lifted them to his lips to place a soft, full kiss first on one, then the other. She could feel the pressure of his kisses through her gloves, but she was taken aback at how much she longed to feel the warmth of his lips and the tickling brush of his mustache against her skin. It was almost overwhelming. She took in a shuddering breath just as he began to move away. "Harry—" she said, leaning toward him. She didn't even know what to say. She just wasn't ready to let him go.

An instant later he was back in front of her, only instead of possessing her hands, he enveloped her face between his great warm palms, bent his head and placed a quick, fleeting kiss on her own surprised lips. Then another, and another, until finally he pressed his mouth into hers and did not pull away.

Something exploded inside Gussie during those brief, transient seconds. She couldn't tell if it came from her head or her heart, her toes, her chest...every inch of her body felt like it had been touched by lightning from each of Harry's kisses. Her eyes remained widened in shock until his lips settled onto hers and did not lift. His thumbs gently grazed her cheeks back and forth until she slowly closed her eyes and leaned into the caress.

Harry pulled back abruptly only to touch his forehead against her own, each of them taking in a breath. Then he raised his head to look at her, eyes darting back and forth between her own. His hands still cradled her cheeks between them. Though his kisses had been soft and quick, he seemed out of breath.

"I'm—I'm sorry, Gussie." He released her and stepped back, running a hand through his hair. "I promise I won't ever do that again. I'm not a nincompoop. I am a complete blackguard. Forgive me."

Gussie could only watch as he turned and walked away from her.

Chapter Nineteen

Perhaps he was a coward for walking away, but it was the only way Harry knew how to rein himself in. If he stayed near Gussie, he would be doing neither of them any favors, even if he tried to mend things. Not that anything could repair the damage he had just done.

He'd thought he could do it again. As he had done regarding the Pact, he'd thought he could assure her that he had no expectations after what had happened at the fountain.

He had almost been successful too. Taking her hands to kiss had crossed a line he had not meant to, but he'd meant it as a farewell of sorts. A farewell to his hopes of having her as his wife. He'd remained in complete control of his aching heart until she had called out to him in such a way...

Something in her voice had snapped any bonds that had been constraining his overwhelming feelings of love and longing, and he had turned back to show her his love the only way he knew how. And by doing so, he had ruined everything.

To add salt to the wound, he could not take the time he really needed to get a hold of himself. He was expected in the dining room by the rest of the party. Expected to be jovial and cheerful, without a care in the world when what he really wished to do was punch something, *anything*. He was so angry with himself for treating Gussie that way.

He had been ready to accept it, respect her wishes. But that was not what had happened, and now there was no doubt in his mind he had lost not just a chance to win her love, but her friendship too. Gussie Stilwell did not like surprises, especially ones that involved close proximity, and what had he done? Not just in this instance, but in their past encounters since he'd returned to England. Pouncing on her and Rosy in the field, swinging her down from the carriage, taking her hand in his when he had noticed her nervous tic, the list went on. How had he ever thought he had been a good friend when he'd kept teasing her so?

Trying time and again to get a laugh out of her or coax her out of her usual, serious nature?

He had to move. He couldn't simply disappear like he wanted to. Not while he was hosting guests. Besides, they would be expecting Gussie too, though Harry did not know if she was in a condition to come. He could not go and look for her, to see if she was well. She would not want him anywhere near her, he was certain. If she did not appear soon after his entrance, he would quietly send Mary out to find her.

Coming up to the dining room, he took in two short, quick breaths, plastered a smile on his face, and opened the door. He did his best to revert to his usual self and hoped that no one caught on to just how much effort it was taking him to keep that pleasant look on his face. He would give Gussie twenty seconds to come in before he would give a hint to Mary.

She came in after seventeen, poised and calm as ever. "Forgive me," she said to the inquiries about her tardiness. "I stepped on my dress coming into the house and tore a flounce. I was only pinning it up."

Harry felt relieved that he had not alarmed her enough that she could not be in company, but aside from looking up at her entrance, he kept his eyes away from her for the rest of her visit.

Oddly enough, it was his mother who engaged her in conversation the most. Gussie's replies were everything civil, if not warm. However much Mrs. Fletcher might take umbrage at her son being rejected, she would certainly think it best in the long run. Harry could see her patience growing thin as she kept conversing with Gussie.

When Mary's phaeton was brought round, all the Fletchers came outside to see them off. Harry handed Mary up into her seat, but before he could get around to do the same to Gussie, an Oakleigh groom was already assisting her before he perched himself on the back of the phaeton. So much the better. Harry wouldn't be surprised if she recoiled from his touch.

Mary gathered up the reins and nodded to the Camrose groom at the horses' heads to release them.

"We shall see you at our ball. Do not forget!" cried Charlotte.

Would Gussie even come to the ball now? Like her reaction to the fish being thrown at her, Harry couldn't imagine her wanting anything to do with him from now on. To think that he and a slimy fish would have so much in common!

He finally dared look Gussie full in the face before the phaeton took her out of sight. Not that it did any good. She could be thinking about the kisses he'd given her or the great pyramids of Giza for all her expression revealed to him.

He and his family turned back to the house. Amy and Charlotte began at once to discuss the dresses and bonnets the Stilwell women had been wearing. Mrs. Fletcher nodded in agreement with their favorable assessments. "You both have a good eye for fashion, my darlings. I am glad they were able to come on such short notice."

Harry, following them into the house, nodded. "You two were very nice to think of inviting them," he said to his sisters.

"They didn't invite them. I did."

Harry stopped and stared at his mother. "You asked them to come? I thought it was Amy's idea."

Mrs. Fletcher tilted her head to the side, thinking on her response. "She was certainly in favor of it, but I raised the subject in the first place. The Stilwells are good society, and it is beneficial to the girls, and to me also. And I think that one's opinion of some people may improve if further acquaintance is actively sought, don't you?"

***

On the way back to Oakleigh, thoughts and feelings were spinning round and round in Gussie like so many swirling dervishes. Harry had kissed her not just once, but six times: once on each hand, and four times on her mouth. The number of kisses she'd thought she would receive in her life had sextupled.

She had wondered what it was like to be kissed several times over the years and always in her dry, calculating manner. In all her mental scenarios, she hadn't taken into account how much moisture might be involved. Especially on Harry's last kiss.

She was sure friends did not kiss friends like that. She was also certain that a man didn't kiss a woman so softly when he was angry and didn't want anything to do with her anymore. It seemed that for all her worrying, the opposite had happened: Harry still loved her, despite the hurt she knew she'd caused him.

Now that she was sure she loved him, this information changed things entirely.

"You're quiet," Mary observed. "Were you terribly uncomfortable there? I didn't see you or Harry speak to each other much."

"I am...well," Gussie said at last, which was true. At least, she thought she *would* be well once she sorted through everything that had just happened. "No, we didn't speak much. But I can't speak right now, dear heart. Will you let me think for a little while?"

Chapter Twenty

The day of the Camrose ball came without any sight of Gussie in the days between. Harry wasn't surprised by this, but not an hour passed by where he did not kick himself for losing her because of his wretched, selfish actions. On top of that, he could not fulfill his promise to his mother to announce an engagement tonight and marry straight after the new year.

He didn't know when he would be able to look at another woman with an eye to matrimony. He had never had his heart broken like this before. This weight of disappointment and sorrow added to his shoulders, already sagging under the burden of his inheritance and the management of all of Camrose, had him feeling very low indeed. How was he to host a whole evening of gaiety under such a burden?

The ball was still some hours away when a footman came into the study bearing a note on a silver tray. Harry, bogged down with papers and diagrams of drainage techniques, took the note and tossed it aside. If the sender hadn't told the footman it was urgent, it could wait until he understood what a tile in the shape of a 'C' had to do with a 'mug' in the diagram he was studying.

Half an hour later, Charlotte came into the room red-eyed and sniffling. "Harry. Amy says that this ribbon makes my face look orange when I wear it in my hair, but it doesn't, does it?"

She held up a blue ribbon and rested it on her cheek, looking at him imploringly. Harry looked back in silence as he mustered up some patience. "Where is Mama? She would know better than I."

"I can't find her. She is in one place then another getting everything ready. Besides, she is too distracted to ask right now. My face isn't orange, is it?"

She took a step closer and leaned over the desk, presenting herself for inspection. Harry tried to disclaim but decided the faster he indulged her, the faster he would be left in peace.

"Put the ribbon down." She obeyed. "Now put it back." Up went the ribbon to her cheek. He pressed his lips and gave a slow nod. "You look exactly the same either way. If you like the color, wear it. No one will say your face is orange. Stop allowing Amy to get a rise out of you."

"There's no difference at all? I don't look better?" Charlotte asked. She looked down, disappointed for some mysterious reason. Then her brow furrowed. "What a crude hand. Who writes notes to you in print?"

Harry's eyes followed his sister's gaze until they rested on the note that had been brought in. He hadn't bothered to look at the direction but now he reached out and turned the note to read it. What he saw nearly made his mouth drop.

That was Gus Stillman's hand.

He took up the note to inspect it more carefully. Yes, he would recognize that plain script anywhere and could match it to every one of the nine letters directed to him in India.

"Is it important?" Charlotte asked.

"No," he replied. "Nothing of consequence to anyone. Probably a message from a tradesman regarding an order for the ball. I've had more of those than I can count, let me tell you. Charlotte, you'll look beautiful in any color you choose, but do run away and allow me to finish my business."

Harry waited a beat after the door latch clicked behind his sister before tearing the wafer off and unfolding the note. Gussie had always written the direction in print as Gus Stillman, but within the missives, her long, scrawling hand was revealed. This note was no different.

Gus Stillman requests a meeting with Sir Harry Fletcher of Camrose Hall at no later than four o' clock at the place on Broadstone land where promises are made.

Harry flipped the note over. That was the entire message. He dug out his watch and checked the time. Three forty-seven. He looked at the note again. *No later than four o' clock...*

A moment later, Harry burst through the doors of his study and made haste to his room, calling out for any servant within earshot to have his horse brought round.

***

Gussie had tucked a little book in the pocket of her habit to while away the time under the birch tree. She did this more out of habit than anything. She knew full well that her racing mind would not concentrate on anything until she saw Harry. If he came, that is.

She had tried to calculate the time just right for her to be fifteen minutes earlier than his expected time. Thirty minutes for the footman to get the note to Camrose. Five minutes for Harry to read it. Ten to twenty minutes for him to finish anything he might be doing. Ten minutes to change and have his horse saddled. Twenty to thirty minutes to get to the birch in the Broadstone fields, assuming his pace would be a smart trot.

So why wasn't he here yet?

Plenty of obstacles could have detained him. He might have been out when her note came. He might have given orders not to be disturbed for any reason. He might...he might not want to come...

She couldn't let herself think about that. It was not yet four o' clock. Five minutes to four was *not* four o' clock.

She looked at her horse, contentedly lipping up any choice bit of the dead brown grass, and decided to wait until four ten. Any later and she would be late in preparing for the ball.

Four ten came and went.

He wasn't coming.

Holding back the tears of disappointment that stung her eyes, Gussie looped the reins over Brutus's head and led him over to the stone wall to mount. Before she reached it however, the sound of pounding hooves in the distance came to her ears. She turned to see a rider galloping up the lane toward the field.

That was Harry's gray, and that was Harry riding him with no hat or gloves. He veered off the road before it went up the rise to where the birch was. Urged on by Harry's voice, the gray jumped the stone wall, its legs tucked neatly under it before continuing up the slope on the same side of the wall as Gussie.

Only when he was a few yards away from her did Harry pull his horse up. Indeed, he was so close that Gussie shrunk back, fearing a collision. "Harry, really!" she cried.

He dismounted, completely winded. Had he galloped the whole way here? He raised a finger, asking her to wait while he took a few deep gasps for breath while she stared at him.

He was here. He had come.

Taking one last breath, he finally said, "Mr. Stillman, forgive my tardiness. I had not expected to hear from you."

Gussie's lips spread into a nervous smile. "Mr. Stillman thought that a request to meet with him would be more agreeable than a request from Gussie."

Harry's eyes lit with amusement. "Is that so? Well, you may inform this Miss Gussie that she was anxious for nothing. I will meet with either of you." He ended on a chuckle, but his face quickly fell into a somber expression. "I am sorry about before. About the kiss."

"Oh, that, well," Gussie said, flustered. She had to hurry. She could feel her nerve slipping away. If he said no, he said no, and she would have to live with that. But she had to tell him. "What if I want to be a nincompoop?" she said in a rush.

Harry blinked. "I beg your pardon, what?"

Gussie took her lips between her teeth. "I didn't mean—what I meant was, there is nothing to apologize for. I didn't mind the kiss. Kisses."

Harry studied her with narrowed eyes, as if he couldn't believe her words. "*Didn't* mind?"

"You surprised me, that is true. I never expected it. I never expected a lot of things. Like you inheriting; like being bound to a Pact that was suddenly fulfilled. When you spoke to me about it that night at the Welbeck's, I said one would have to be a nincompoop to put any store by what we did when we were children, remember?"

Harry nodded slowly. "I remember. You also said one would be a nincompoop to accept such a proposal made by a foolish man."

Gussie bristled. "I did not say that."

"You did."

"The nincompoop part, yes. The foolish man? No."

Harry lifted a hand, signaling a touch. "Fair enough. And now, you are saying that you...want to be a nincompoop after all?"

The dawning realization on his face gave her enough courage to go on. "What I am trying to say is that I have been a nincompoop this entire time. I had no wish for anything to change. I would never marry and would be happy in my little country cottage surrounded by my books and my lovely walks and still be best friends with Harry Fletcher."

Harry looked at her intently, talking a step toward her. "But?"

Heart racing, she took a step toward him. "But I think I can imagine my life going down a different path. One with more company. Perpetual company, in fact. I can imagine it, and I have been." She looked up into Harry's eyes. "If it is too late, tell me at once, but while I haven't been very wise, or kind, I can imagine what a life would look like by your side, and I rather like it. It still frightens me, a lot. I know you have promises to keep. I couldn't rush into this, but if you still love me so, so dearly, I believe I love you so, so, *so* dearly, my friend."

She ended on a hitched breath that was immediately muffled by Harry's coat as he enfolded her in his arms. "My darling friend," he said above her. "You mean it, truly?"

Gussie pressed her face deeper into his chest and nodded. He responded by squeezing her tighter. "Will you take this ridiculous hat off?" he said through a chuckle.

She laughed as she felt his hand tug and pull at her bonnet, which was firmly attached to her hair with a pin. Her deft fingers soon found it and pulled it out. "Try now."

Off went the hat, flying in the air as Harry tossed it aside. He nestled his cheek on the top of her head. "That's better," he murmured into her hair.

Gussie had never been held this way in her life, so closely by a man. It was a lot to experience all in a few short moments, but she remained in his arms, wishing to feel every feeling that came with this new encounter. "I'm sorry it took me so long to realize it," she whispered.

Harry's hand stroked the back of her head. "I'm sorry I acted so rashly. I knew you didn't love me, but I'd fallen in love with you so many months ago that I let my heart run away with me sometimes, and that wasn't fair to you."

She pulled away just enough to look up at him. "Did it happen on the ship?"

He smiled and shook his head. "That is where it solidified, but I think it happened soon after John died. Even before I'd gotten word about my cousin's death. Your letters acted like a balm to me. And when I found out I'd inherited Camrose, I knew I wanted to get back to you. Not because you assuaged my grief. The Pact didn't even cross my mind until I boarded the ship. I wanted to get back to you because I loved you."

Gussie looked at him, amazed. "You loved me all that time?"

His soft smile and the tender light in his eye made her heart do the most spectacular acrobatics. "But Harry, understand me. I love you, truly, but this is all so new...it's not as if I can marry you tomorrow. I will need time. I am not any less afraid of, well, the things I mentioned to you before. Forgive me, but I will need a lot of time before marriage could be—"

Harry lifted his hand and rested a finger on her lips. "You shall have all the time you need. As for these fears, there is only one that I am powerless to help you with. The others, I promise you, are not as frightening as you have been made to think. And I won't marry you tomorrow—well, don't mistake me, I would marry you today if I could, but I want to marry the Gussie who is ready to marry me. The Gussie whom I will have to catch up with as she bolts to the altar. I'll wait for her. However long it takes, I'll wait. And while I wait, I'll make her laugh, tell her she is beautiful and caring and clever every single day...and by the look on your face, better make it only once a week, or you'll jilt me before a month has gone by."

Gussie laughed at that. She had a feeling she would be laughing more than she had ever done before. But she grew solemn once more. "What about your mother? Her hopes for a speedy engagement and marriage for you?"

Harry hummed, contemplating. "I don't think she will be opposed to the idea as much as you fear. A long courtship will help the two of you understand one another better. I believe that time is only needed for her to love you, if you allow her to."

"I wish to know her better too. I cannot promise I won't run away to my room when I need solitude, but I will excuse myself with the utmost civility when it happens."

Harry laughed and tightened his arms around her. "And that acquaintance shall progress as slowly as you like too. You shall name the day we become engaged, and the day we shall marry, whenever that may be. I'll wait. I'll wait for twenty years if I must. It—it wouldn't take twenty years, would it?"

Gussie cocked her head to one side, thinking. "No. I shouldn't think so."

Harry nodded, relieved. "I am glad to hear it. Though I would wait, regardless. But in the meantime, may I kiss you?"

Epilogue

Rome, Spring 1816

The crisp click of Harry's boots on the marble floors sent Gussie's lips up into an expectant smile. She nestled back into her pillows and brought her chocolate to her lips for one more sip before Harry opened the door to her—no, *their*—chambers.

"Still in bed?" Harry asked, a teasing light in his eye. "I was sure you'd be halfway to the catacombs without me by now."

He strode over to the bed. Placing his arms on either side of her, he bent his head down to her. Gussie lowered her cup of chocolate and tilted her face up to meet him halfway, pressing a soft, full kiss on his lips which he returned with an eager tenderness that sent chills through her.

When he pulled back, he passed his tongue over his lips. "Mmm. I think I like this Italian chocolate more than our English chocolate now."

Gussie chuckled and held the cup out to him. "There is a difference, though I can't quite tell what they do to it. I shall have to ask my maid to find out. Have a taste."

Harry pushed the cup back toward her. "I will."

Catching on, Gussie pursed her lips mischievously before taking another sip, letting her tongue roll the hot liquid to and fro. Just after she swallowed, Harry's mouth came to hers, and taste the chocolate he did.

Eighteen months ago, Gussie had never thought a kiss like this could exist, or that she would enjoy such an experience. Harry's kisses during their courtship and engagement had hinted at such passions as time went by, but it wasn't until she'd become Lady Augusta Fletcher, not a fortnight ago, that she'd begun discovering just how enjoyable kissing one's husband could be.

Wanting his opinion to be fully informed, Gussie took one hand off her cup and threaded her fingers through his hair, pressing him in closer.

Harry would have fully obliged had there not been a full cup of steaming chocolate between them. He pulled back with a sigh. "It would be a shame to let it cool. Tell me instead what's on the docket today besides surrounding ourselves with skulls."

Adjusting herself so he could sit comfortably on the edge of the bed beside her, Gussie said, "The catacombs are not until this afternoon. This morning it is to be the Roman Forum and the Colosseum. Then there is the opera tonight. It is a new one, *the Barber of Seville*. Oh, but before that, I want to continue my sketches of the Trevi Fountain this evening. I'm going to make watercolors for all my sisters."

"Amy and Charlotte will love theirs, I'm sure. When will you write them next?"

"Oh, not until I have at least a week of Rome to talk of first," Gussie replied. "I'll send letters so crossed and recrossed that they will know I am enjoying myself. How was your morning stroll? When Alice brought my chocolate, she told me the day looked to be fine, but what do you think?"

"See for yourself, sleeping beauty." Harry rose and walked over to the window covered by heavy, intricately designed brocade curtains. With a quick flick of his wrists, he swished them back. Bright, airy sunlight spilled into the room, and Gussie's eyes met with a view of the Fontana di Trevi from their quaint lodgings in a corner of the Piazza di Trevi. The sun only brightened half the magnificent fountain now with its morning rays. Gussie would never tire of looking at it.

Harry looked back at her. "Do you think we shall do here? Is a month enough time for us to explore before moving on to Naples?"

Gussie sighed contentedly. "Oh, I should think so, if we keep to my itinerary."

Harry blew out a breath from puffed cheeks as he walked back to her. "I read over that again this morning. If I am to keep up with you, I'd better have two helpings of everything at breakfast. And coffee. Lots of coffee." He took his place at the edge of the bed again. "But don't worry, love. You shall have all the time you need to enjoy it here."

The mention of time sent a warm glow radiating through Gussie's chest. There had been times in the past eighteen months when Gussie wondered at the patience Harry showed as they courted. More patience than she often showed herself. Though there had been seasons of frustration and uncertainty (especially when news of Napoleon's escape set off another war), the passage of time, filled with many a conversation during their private country land rides, plenty of reading, and even a few interviews with a discreet doctor, had done wonderful things to not cure her fears, but calm them enough for her to face the future with anticipation and hope.

She put her chocolate down on the breakfast tray, pushed the tray away, and gathered Harry up into her arms. "You already gave me all the time I needed. Harry, I love you so much. I don't know what I've done to deserve you."

Harry pressed himself tighter against her. "Plenty, believe me."

"You waited so long..."

"But you were there to keep me company. The time you took to make sure this was what you really wanted was time well spent. I wouldn't have missed a day of it. I love you, Gussie Stilwell."

She pushed him away to arm's length. "It's Lady Fletcher to you. Don't ever call me Gussie Stilwell again." She pressed a finger to his chest with each word to make sure her point hit home.

He let out a laugh. "You won't hear any arguments from me, *Lady Fletcher*."

"That is more like it, *Sir Harry*." She pulled him back to her for a kiss. Then another, and another.

"Shouldn't we get down to breakfast, love?" Harry murmured against her lips.

Still kissing him, Gussie put a hand on his chest and felt around until she reached the pocket of his waistcoat under his jacket. She pulled out his watch and broke away only enough to look at the time. "According to my itinerary, we still have twenty minutes before breakfast."

"Do we, indeed?" he asked, taking the watch from her and replacing it in his pocket. He then moved his hand to the nape of her neck, pulling her in for a deeper kiss. "And what does this itinerary say to do in the meantime?"

"Funny thing, I left it blank," she said in between kisses. "We shall have to think of something. Any ideas?"

Thank you for reading! As an enthusiast for history and especially the Regency Era, I have done my best to stay true and accurate to the events and culture of the period through my research. I'd like to thank the Historymakers Group for sharing their findings and knowledge with me and I hope I can in turn share the knowledge I'm gaining with others.

If you enjoyed this book and want to sign up for my newsletter to receive updates about upcoming works, click here[1]. Reviews (the good, bad and the ugly!) are always read and appreciated.

Other works by Amanda Panhorst
<u>The Langham Line</u>
The Wife of Walraven[2]
Letty's Last Love[3]
<u>Reluctant Titles</u>
The Earl from Eastbend[4]
The Baronet from Bombay
<u>Novellas</u>
Chasing Desford[5]

---

1.   https://amandapanhorst.com/

2. https://www.amazon.com/Wife-Walraven-Regency-Romance-Langham-ebook/dp/ B08JLK1K6T/ref=sr_1_1?crid=1ZG1M1V23XWBM&keywords=the+wife+of+wal-raven&qid=1650290232&sprefix=the+wife+of+walrave%2Caps%2C266&sr=8-1

3. https://www.amazon.com/gp/product/B08YJB-WRZF?ref_=dbs_p_pwh_rwt_anx_cl_1&storeType=ebooks

4. https://www.amazon.com/gp/product/B09FLBDDRG/ref=dbs_a_def_rwt_bibl_vppi_i0

5. https://www.amazon.com/gp/product/B08HQ7W1PS/ref=dbs_a_def_rwt_bibl_vppi_i1